The Shadow's Shine

The Summer of 1985

Teri Leigh

The Shadow's Shine
Copyright © 2020 by TeriLeigh LLC

ISBN 978-0-9859643-9-9

Dedication

for my Hobbit
who taught me how to laugh in the dark

and

to MFunk
for reminding me that writing is my first love

Table of Contents

CHAPTER ONE

Letting Go

It was the windiest day of the year, the last day of school. My last day of sixth grade. The entire elementary school burst out the doors of the school to the field between the school and the playground. Everyone was excited—so excited that as much as the grown-ups yelled at us kids to walk, not run, we couldn't help ourselves. We fast-walked into a skip, a run, and back to a fast-walk to form lines behind a handful of helium tanks. Collectively, at $1.00 for each balloon, the school had raised nearly $5000 for our balloon launch for Save the Children.

"What color balloons would you like?" one of the room parents asked me when I got to the front of the line.

"Purple, please," I said, handing her my ticket with the number 13 written prominently on the back in black sharpie.

"All of them?" she said as she counted out the strings of thirteen purple balloons.

"Yup."

"As you wish," she said, handing me 13 strings attached to 13 purple balloons.

"You're so predictable," Teddy said, winking at me as he asked the room parent to give him 10 blue balloons and one white one.

"I can't help it. I'm a purple person. People who love purple LOVE purple," I said while waiting for him. "Besides, purple is the color of magic."

"Purple is such a girl color."

"Well then, it's a good thing that I'm a girl."

"Make that nine blue, one white, and one purple," Teddy said, smiling at me with his Teddy twinkle.

"As you wish," the room mother said again.

Looking up at my 13 balloons as I waited for Teddy to get his stash, I counted in my head 13 wishes. Six wishes of things I wanted to let go of. Six wishes for things I wanted. And then one wish, the most important one. That one, I didn't really completely understand.

"What did you wish for?" Teddy asked as we walked towards the sixth grade section by the basketball courts.

"Stupid stuff really," I said.

"C'mon. I'll tell you mine if you tell me yours," he prodded.

"You first."

"I wished that junior high turns out to be better than this hellhole," he laughed.

"This place wasn't that bad."

"No, you're right, it wasn't. And you're stalling."

"Okay, I wished for world peace and an end to all hunger."

"Liar."

"I'm not lying."

He rolled his eyes at me.

"I forgot for a second who I was talking to. Of course you did."

"What else did you wish for?" I asked.

"Honestly," he said, his tone turning somber, "I wished that Angry Man would stop being so angry."

"You haven't talked about Angry Man in a long time."

"I know. And I'm not talking about him anymore now either. Your turn."

"Okay, but you have to promise you won't think it's stupid."

"I promise."

"Cross your heart?"

"Hope to die and stick a needle in my eye."

"Okay." I took a breath. "I wish for an adventure so big that I get to feel things I've never felt before, bigger things, more grown-up things."

"I don't think that's stupid at all," Teddy said.

"Really?"

"No, it's deep. And I get it."

"Thanks."

"Can I uncross my heart, hope to live, and take the needle out of my eye now?"

"I suppose so."

Twenty minutes later, the crowd quieted down as Mr. Burnett, the school principal, stood at the podium holding his hand up on the air, the universal signal for silence. He talked for a little bit about the famine in Ethiopia, and some mumbo jumbo about hope and giving back to those in need.

A gust of wind distracted me when it blew my 13 purple balloons into a sparring match, like a bunch of boxing gloves warming up for a big fight. I almost lost my balance.

Mrs. Evenrude, the school choir teacher, took the podium and directed us in singing *We Are the World,* as we had practiced in choir class for weeks. Select soloists from each class stepped forward to the mic while the rest of us sung along with the chorus.

About the time Tracey Jones stepped forward in her full Cyndi Lauper costume, I felt someone bump me from behind. When I turned to look, no one was there.

I stopped singing.

That's when I saw them. Well, I didn't really SEE them. Rather, I *sensed* them: two shadowy figures weaving their way through the crowd of children. They were there, but not really, just shadows in my peripheral vision that disappeared when I shifted my focus to try look at them directly. I didn't dare alert my friends to what I saw. Not even Teddy. They'd think I was crazy. Heck, I thought maybe I *was* going crazy.

The Shadows worked their way to the edge of the crowd and stopped on either side of Old Mrs. Schmidt, our former kindergarten teacher, who was retiring after 50 years of teaching five-year-olds how to read. If I looked directly at Mrs. Schmidt, the shadows disappeared. But if I adjusted my focus to look at the swings just beyond her, they reappeared. I relaxed my eyes like I was looking at one of those 3-D pictures, hoping the shadows might materialize into a clearer shape or form.

They did.

They wore heavy, hooded cloaks, so I couldn't see their faces very clearly. They were about twice the size of Mrs. Schmidt, maybe 10 feet tall. One of them had heavy chains around his neck. That one placed a hand on Mrs. Schmidt's shoulder, which came to about the height of his own waist. The other one had turned his back to her and faced the crowd, hands on his hips, as if he were standing guard.

I suspected she sensed them, because she physically winced under the pressure of the Shadow's hand on her shoulder. She stared up at her balloons with this odd look on her face. While I expected she would look scared, she didn't. Instead, she looked, well, exhilarated.

I couldn't tell if she was looking at the Shadow or if she saw right through him to her balloons. The Shadow took her arm by the wrist, the one holding the balloons, and raised it as high above her head as it could go. He fastened one of his shackles to her forearm. And she smiled, this odd smile, like she felt comforted.

Then I got that heebie-jeebie feeling. A cold tingle down my back, starting at the nape of my neck and stopping at the bottom of my shoulder blades. Like someone was watching me.

It was the other Shadow.

He stared right at me.

I blinked and rubbed my eyes with my thumb and middle finger. When I opened them again, he was gone. But as soon as I relaxed my eyes, he appeared again. Only this time, I could see him more clearly, as a sunbeam caught his face just right from under his hood. He had a wrinkled and weathered old man face, scraggly eyebrows, and thin lips. He looked right in my eyes. His lips moved as if he were speaking, but I didn't hear him. He was too far away. But I *felt* a warm breathy whisper in my ear and down my neck, as if he were standing right behind me.

Was that the wind? It couldn't be . . .

Too many things happened all at once.

Mr. Burnett, the school principal, dropped his arms.

Thousands of balloons floated into the cloudless sky.

Everyone squealed in excitement.

The Shadow released Mrs. Schmidt's arm from his grip.

One of my purple balloons popped.

Mrs. Schmidt collapsed to the ground.

I felt a cold, bony hand on my shoulder. I knew it was his. I didn't dare look. It was heavy, heavier than I could bear. I fell to my knees, with my purple balloons still clutched in my fist, my fingernails digging into my palm. I opened my mouth to scream, but no sound came out. Nothing did. Not even air. I choked on my own not-breath.

"It's almost time . . . for you to know me."

The Shadow grabbed the strings of my balloons and pulled them out of my fist, releasing them for me.

"I'll teach you how to let go."

CHAPTER TWO

The Visitation

"Her mouth looks weird," Kevin said. We stood in the back corner of the funeral home, me and my three friends, Kevin Tomkins, and Teddy and his twin brother Tommy James. We stared at Mrs. Schmidt's open casket which was in the front of the room. She didn't look at all like we remembered her. Her lips were thinner and wider, pressed into a creepy joker's grin. Her skin had a yellow, shiny tinge to it, and her jaw seemed to be accentuated more than the rest of her face.

Kevin was too excited about seeing a dead body for the first time to keep his voice hushed to the right level between whisper and normal. His words spilled over his lips like the foam of a root beer float.

"Maybe it froze that way after all those years of dealing with brat kids like you," Teddy whispered, nudging an elbow into Kevin's ribs. "Clean yourself up, you freak."

Crumbs from the cracker Kevin had snatched from the vending machine in the entryway were stuck in the corner of his mouth and between his teeth. He tried to pull his suit jacket sleeve over his hand to use as a napkin, but it snagged on the too-big watch dangling from his wrist.

"Whose is that?" Tommy asked while Kevin stuffed the watch inside his sleeve so he could successfully wipe his mouth from ear to ear.

"My mom said this is a special occasion, so I get to wear my grandad's watch," Kevin said proudly, holding up his wrist to show off the watch. His smile revealed clean lips, but saliva-soaked bits of cracker were wedged between most of his front teeth.

"You idiots." My older brother Dave walked up to us, deliberately blocking our view of the casket. "Her mouth looks like that because it's sewn shut."

"Why is it sewn shut?" Kevin asked, biting into another cracker.

"When people die, the muscles in their jaws can't hold their mouths closed anymore, so they have to sew the lips shut to keep the mouth closed." Dave said in his big-brother-I-know-better-than-you voice.

"Bull!" Kevin said, sticking his tongue in his lower lip, making a face at Dave.

"I'm serious," Dave said, his whisper growing to a low mumble.

"Next you're gonna tell me that dead bodies fart and burp too," Kevin huffed.

"Actually, they do," Dave said. "After someone dies, the muscles that hold the piss and shit in relax, and it just comes out."

"Bull crap. A dead body can't piss and shit," Tommy whispered.

"Prove it," Kevin challenged.

"Fine. I will. I'll find the funeral home director," Dave said.

"Tommy James, watch your language," Mrs. James said, her voice quivering with the energy of too much caffeine. "Your father would not be pleased."

"Sorry, Mom," Teddy and Tommy said in unison as they dropped their chins.

"Let's go pay our respects properly," Mrs. James said.

Both boys followed their mother to the open casket. Tommy kept his head down low enough that he could avoid looking at the corpse at all. But Teddy stood tall, his hands clasped behind his back, leaning in a little. He looked oddly curious.

"Speaking of pissing, I gotta go," Kevin announced as he marched towards the bathroom. I tried to say "okay," but ever since we had entered the funeral home, I hadn't been able to speak because my tongue felt too big for my mouth. All I could do was give Kevin an awkward wave.

I scanned the room for my brothers and my parents, but my eyes couldn't focus enough to see or recognize the faces of any individual. Rather, I just saw an undulating blob of blackness. I found myself suddenly alone, and oddly hypersensitive, amidst a sea of faceless Lutheran mourners dressed in black.

An older woman took a half-step back from the circle of women and bumped my shoulder, and I lost my balance.

"Oh, my dear, I'm so sorry," she said as she grasped my forearm to help steady me.

It's okay, you didn't bump me that hard.

My words stuck in my throat and never left my mouth.

"I didn't see you there."

I smiled awkwardly, pulling my arm out of her grip to cross my arms tightly, clutching my notebook to my chest.

"Were you one of Hilda's students?"

I nodded.

"I'm sorry for your loss," she said.

My tongue was stuck on the roof of my mouth. So, I just nodded again.

She turned and disappeared into the black sea, leaving me in a heavy cloud of her obnoxious perfume, which made my eyes water to the point of actual tears.

Great, now people are gonna think I'm crying over my old kindergarten teacher.

A middle-aged man squeezed by me. His suit jacket brushed against my upper arm. While the suit jacket looked soft, it felt more like hairbrush bristles being dragged harshly against the tender skin of my arm. I gasped, and immediately felt self-conscious about the noise. Instinctively, I grasped at my arm where his jacket had grazed me.

Why did that hurt?

"Pardon me," he said, looking down at me with kindness in his eyes. I looked back up at him, my eyes still wet from the sting of the perfume.

"Is this your first funeral, sweetheart?" he said. He offered me a tissue he had pulled from his inside jacket pocket.

I nodded, using the tissue to blot my eyes.

I wish I could tell him that I'm not really crying.

"May we all find comfort in the fact that she's in a better place now, with our Lord and Savior," he said with a breathy voice just above a whisper.

I nodded.

He placed his hand on my shoulder, and I winced under the pressure of it, just like Mrs. Schmidt had with the Shadow. He kept his hand there. I didn't like the feeling, and suddenly felt dizzy.

"Pastor Benson?" A woman wearing a black pillbox hat with a mesh veil framing her face diverted his attention. The veil made her face look fuzzy, out of focus, yet at the same time it drew my eye to her facelessness. The pastor lifted his hand from my shoulder and reached to hold her hand in both of his.

"Pardon me," he said to me as he turned toward her.

Oh thank goodness.

As he spoke with the veiled woman, I squeezed behind the circle of older women and sat down in a mauve velvet armchair in the corner.

You don't see me.

I watched as he looked back to where I had been standing. His eyes darted in search of my disappeared form.

You don't see me.

He turned his gaze back to the veiled woman. I exhaled, a sigh of relief. The same trick I used in class when I didn't want the teacher to call on me had worked here. I made a mental note to myself to practice this power of invisibility in more places.

Curling my legs underneath me, I opened my notebook and started writing down all the overused meaningless phrases that hovered in the air like stale cigarette smoke. The Midwestern niceties seeped out of the mouths of the mourners and wove themselves into the dark green, mauve, and burgundy floral patterns of the funeral home wallpaper.

> I'm sorry for your loss.
> She's in a better place now.
> She is with our Lord and Savior.
> How sad for her dear sister.
> What a tragic way to go.
> It's a blessing that she passed so quickly.
> Thank the Lord she didn't suffer.

I furtively wrote, my pen capturing each phrase, pinning them to the pages of my notebook like a bulletin board. When I ran out of phrases, I started a new page at the back of my journal, the last page, and started writing random questions about death and dying.

> Did she see a light?
> What does the light feel like?
> How come the things people say about death feel so fake?
> Why am I so sensitive to touch and smell right now?

I filled the whole last page of my journal with questions, then turned the page inward and continued to write more. I filled up two and a half more pages from the back page inward.

> What's the difference between grief and sadness?
> What's the difference between sadness and sorrow?
> Why do people feel the need to display dead bodies?
> When she died, why did she have that exhilarated look on her face?
> Is it possible to not be afraid of death?
> Who were those shadows?
> Why were there two of them?

The more questions I wrote, the heavier my breath got. It seemed to match the mumble of the mourners, a rumbling vibration of the inner walls of my chest. The air felt thick in my lungs, making my heartbeat heavy, like a deep, vibrating drum. Eventually the density inside me drowned out the voices in the room. I wanted to squint my ears to hear better, but my ears felt filled with cotton, and my tongue went dry. My lungs and nose tingled with pins-and-needles numbness. My eyes got lost in the swirls of the wallpaper and all sound was muffled to complete silence. The wallpaper gradually faded, and my vision tunneled to black.

Everything in the room evaporated.

But the cold stayed.

That's how I knew it was him. The cold. It felt just like that gust of wind at the balloon release. It wasn't icy cold, or shivery cold, it was this unbearably penetrating wet-cold. Paralyzing.

I didn't see him.

I didn't hear him.

Rather, I *felt* him.

And then,

I *smelled* him.

The Shadow.

The odor was unlike anything I had ever smelled before. If cold had a scent, this was it. Bitter. Sharp. Pungent. Acrid. Even as I exhaled, I could smell it through my tastebuds. I didn't dare open my eyes, even though I thought I could. I didn't want to see him, not this close. The Shadow was scary enough from across the school playground. Now I felt his frigid presence looming over me.

He cupped the back of my head with one hand while he dragged a fingernail down the back of my skull, the back of my neck, to the space between my shoulder blades. He then pressed his forehead into mine, exhaling his bitter vapor breath over my mouth and nose. My lungs seized. A toxic burning permeated my chest cavity, and I was overwhelmed by a familiar-but-not sensation of nose hairs freezing in 40-below-zero temperatures. Cold air whooshed through the unzipped space of my upper back, flooding my heart and lungs. It took my breath away completely.

"I hope we can be friends, Alex."

He pulled his hands away, dragging his fingers through my hair like a comb. When the last wisp of my hair dropped from his fingers, sensation and function returned to my body. I was able to open my eyes, but I couldn't focus them. Through my blurry peripheral vision, I watched the Shadow float through the sea of black jackets and dresses.

The volume of the room slowly turned back up to a low rumble.

"You okay Sis?" Dave palmed the top of my head like a basketball and shook it, shaking me awake from the nothingness into a world of something-ness. I swallowed, still unable to speak.

Had I just passed out?

Is this what fainting feels like?

I shivered, my teeth chattering a bit. Looking up at my older brother, relieved to find he had zero resemblance to the Shadow, I nodded.

"You're sitting underneath the air conditioning vent, silly."

"Oh." I was surprised by the monosyllable that fell out of my mouth.

"The funeral home director was consoling some crying lady, I think it was Mrs. Schmidt's sister."

"Oh."

"I saw all your goofball friends heading out back a minute ago. I think they were gonna walk home."

"Oh."

I looked at the door, still dazed.

"You gonna go with them?"

I nodded and walked toward the door.

Still shivering, I went outside. It was about to rain, and I welcomed the muggy heat of summer as I held the door open for an older couple walking in from the parking lot. The dense warmth enveloped me like a protective wool blanket.

"I'm so sorry for your loss," the man said as he took the door from me. His voice was stoic, his face emotionless.

"Prepare yourself," the woman said, her voice equally monotone, speaking to no one in particular as she walked through the door. "Death always comes in threes."

Off in the distance, leaning up against a brown station wagon, the Shadow nodded at me. Though he was far away, I heard him again, as if he were right next to me.

"The summer heat feels good, doesn't it?"

I nodded.

"You're very special, Alex. You feel all the things they won't let themselves feel."

Like a movie flashback, I re-felt a series of visions and sensations I'd had inside the funeral home.

The haunting image of the sewn-shut mouth of my dead kindergarten teacher.

Mrs. James's over-caffeinated voice.

The obnoxious perfume cloud.

The faceless veiled woman.

The hairbrush bristles on my forearm.

The heavy weight of the pastor's hand on my shoulder.

The Shadow's hand cupping the back of my head.

And then the sky opened and released big, slobbery wet tears, the kind of rain that soaks you faster than a shower with extra-strong water pressure. I stood under a too-small umbrella, staring out at the Shadow.

"You have a lot more to feel, Alex. But don't worry, I'll be here with you through it all."

I don't know why, but I nodded.

CHAPTER THREE

Mud Sledding

I found Teddy and Tommy huddled under a giant umbrella standing at the top of the hill behind the funeral home. They were staring down the wooded hillside toward our backyards, contemplating whether to brave the ragged, woodsy hill, or walk the long way home.

"Where's Kevin?" Teddy asked.

I shrugged my shoulders.

Dammit, I still can't speak.

"Look what I found!" Kevin hollered, running at us across the back lawn of the funeral home. He held up four king-sized, heavy-duty garbage bags, two in each hand and wearing a fifth as a cape tied around his neck. All five bags fluttered and rippled in the wind.

"Where did you find those?" Tommy asked.

"In the bottom of the garbage bin in the bathroom," Kevin said, looking like a wet penguin in his drenched black dress suit.

"So you dug in the trash?" Tommy asked, and Kevin rolled his eyes.

"Does it really matter how I got 'em? I thought we could go sledding!"

"It's the first weekend in June," Tommy said. "You idiot, there's something called SNOW required for sledding,"

"Who needs snow when we have MUD!"

He smoothed out the garbage bags, four in a row, and plopped himself down on one of them.

"C'mon, you losers!"

"Let's go!" Tommy said, jumping onto one of the garbage bags.

"Hell no," Teddy said, planting his foot on Tommy's garbage bag so Tommy couldn't move. "Let me make myself clear. We. Are. Not. The Goonies."

"C'mon!" Tommy pleaded.

"Father would *not* be pleased," Teddy warned with a no-nonsense look in his eye.

Why was Teddy being like this?

"You're such a buzz-kill, Bro."

"Alex? Are you coming?" Kevin asked.

I shook my head.

"Fine. Have it your way. I'm going! This is totally worth a week of house arrest and no Twinkies!" Kevin said. "Tommy, gimme a push!"

As he scooted his butt a few feet, Tommy looped his arm around a tree, planted his foot firmly in the middle of Kevin's back and gave him a solid foot shove.

"Have fun, Chunk!" Tommy hollered, calling Kevin by the nickname we gave him after we became obsessed with *The Goonies*.

"Chunk wasn't with them when they went down the waterslide," Teddy said.

"Buzzkill," Tommy muttered.

Not six feet down the hill Kevin's garbage bag snagged on a tree root. He scooted some more until he caught another patch of mud and skidded another four feet down. The garbage bag snagged on another branch, which tore off a big chunk. At first he tried to hold the two pieces of garbage bag together, but his efforts were unsuccessful, so he eventually ditched the bag altogether, turned himself sideways and started log rolling.

"You lost your shoe!" Tommy hollered down to Kevin.

"I DON'T CARE!" Kevin hollered back.

The sock of Kevin's shoeless foot dangled from his toes, flopping with every roll.

Teddy and Tommy started laughing and pointing. I clutched my belly, trying my best to muffle the giggles.

Halfway down the hill, Kevin got up and started trudging back up the muddy hill. He looked like a swamp monster covered in mud and leaves from head to toe. Several leaves stuck in the matted, sloppy, dark curls of his hair, looking like awkward antennae.

I couldn't stop the laughs. They spilled out of me like rocks out of a giant bucket, plopping into a lake. One after another, sounds tumbled out of me until I was doubled over, both arms wrapped around my belly. The jolting shudder of my shoulders shrugged off the lingering weight of the pastor's hand. Wetness pushed out of my eyes again, washing away the sting of the obnoxious perfume.

Kevin picked up his shoe and hopped on one foot trying to put it back on. That didn't go so well for him, as he took a digger and slipped another several feet back down. When he stopped sliding, instead of putting his shoe back on, he took the other one off and stuffed both his socks inside the shoes.

"Catch!" One at a time, he threw the shoes up the hill toward us.

"That was a weak-ass throw, dude!" Teddy said as the shoes landed a good eight feet short of us.

"I'll throw them again when I get up that far." Kevin huffed as he stopped to catch his breath. He plastered a look of fierce determination on his face, coupled with a giant grin. As he started again to walk back up the hill barefoot, grabbing tree limbs and trunks with each step, his joker-like grin looked faintly like Mrs. Schmidt's morbid mouth.

And I found that the funniest of all.

There was no stopping the heavy waterfall of laughs falling out of me. In order to stop from peeing my pants, I squatted to the ground, clutching my belly, laughing harder than I ever remembered laughing before in my life. I gasped for breath between silent laughs and snorts. Before I realized it, Teddy and Tommy were no longer laughing at Kevin, but at me.

"THAT! WAS! SO! MUCH! FUN!!" Kevin exclaimed, huffing a breath between each word, when he got back to the top of the hill. It wasn't until he caught his breath that my laughter softened into hiccuping giggles.

And then, for the first time since before I entered the funeral home, I found my voice.

"Kevin! Your Grandad's watch!" I said, pointing at his muddy, but bare, wrist.

"Oh shit! Oh Shit! OH SHIT!" the joker grin left, replaced with guilt and fear. "You gotta help me find it!"

While he was pacing and oh-shitting all over the funeral home lawn, I grabbed one of the unused garbage bags, ripped holes in the bottom for my head and arms, and pulled it on like a poncho. Then, I took another one and poked holes in the bottom and stepped my legs through the holes. I used the laces of Kevin's shoes as a belt to cinch the two bags around my waist.

"What are you doing?" Teddy asked.

His eyes went dark.

I'd seen that look on Teddy's face before, but he was always able to blink it away in less than a second. This time, it lingered longer. It hovered like a visor over his sullen face.

What was Teddy that afraid of?

For the second time that day, the zipper between my shoulder blades opened, and I felt the cold rush of wet air gush between the back of my lungs. In that frozen-time moment when Teddy's eyes went dark, I didn't just observe, I felt. A shiver and tingle went down my spine all the way to my tailbone.

Only this time, my world didn't go dark.

Rather, everything went bright.

Squintingly bright.

The bright overtook my face and somehow my face became the inverse mirror image of Teddy's. His frown, my smile. His dark eyes, my bright eyes. His furrowed forehead, my lifted eyebrows.

I gotta find that watch!

"I'm goin' in!" I said, handing him my umbrella, notebook, and shoes.

"Are you freakin' crazy?"

"Yup."

"You're never gonna find it down there."

"Watch me!" I said.

"Nah. We gotta get home," Teddy said, making a face at Tommy.

"Suit yourself," I said as Teddy and Tommy started walking back across the funeral home lawn. Kevin set to work poking holes in the remaining garbage bag and stepping his legs through it as I had. By the time he finished, I was already marching down the hill.

It wasn't long before I was on my butt, sliding down the path Kevin had plowed in his wake. Scanning the terrain with my eyes for the watch, I dragged my hands on the earth beside me as I slid. As I neared the place where Kevin had torn his first garbage bag, my descent slowed. And then everything slowed to slower than slow motion, like the Earth stopped rotating on its axis for a moment. The steepness of the hill had me laying almost flat on my back, my head lifted, one leg kicking up in the air.

That's when I found it.

My right hand caught a small tree trunk, and my left hand landed on the torn piece of Kevin's garbage bag, still caught on the broken-off tree branch. Through the plastic, I felt the perfectly round shape of the watch face resting on its linked wristband. I reached under the bag and clasped the watch in my fist.

Once again, my unzipping opened.

But this time was different.

It wasn't scary or cold.

It was comforting and warm.

All the feelings and weirdness of the day just evaporated, as if they had never happened. Time stopped, just for a moment. I felt utter contentment. Laying there on the soft, wet earth, I closed my eyes for a moment and breathed in the scent of fresh rain. When I opened my eyes again, a heavy raindrop landed in my right eye, and everything blurred. I squinted my eyes shut to push away the wetness.

Then I smelled him.

He helped me find the watch!

The Shadow.

Only this time his bitter scent had a tinge of sweetness. It reminded me vaguely of the inside of my grandpa's closet, a mix of Old Spice and slightly stale cigar breath.

When I opened my eyes again, before I could focus them, I saw him, sitting over me, with a grandfatherly smile on his lips.

I blinked, and he was gone.

The scent of fresh rain returned.

As suddenly as the rain had started, it stopped. The downpour was over, without even a spit or sputter remaining. Protected under the canopy of the leaves, I looked up through the clouds and saw the sun working to burn its way back into view.

"KEVIN! I FOUND IT!" I yelled as I punched my fist up to the sky like a superhero.

CHAPTER FOUR

Weightlessness

It rained every day for nearly a week. Teddy, Tommy and I played marathon games of Monopoly and MPBA Baseball while Kevin served his house arrest sentence for ruining his new suit. The first day of severe clear, the same day Kevin got off house arrest, we all met up after breakfast at the Stink House.

The Stink House was a small, red-brick building, less than eight feet high, that anchored the other end of our cul de sac. We never really understood its purpose as kids, and only learned later in life about the workings of the sewer system and the need for a pump house. We just knew it smelled like shit. Some days were worse than others. Those really hot days when the humidity hung in the air like a wet rag on your face, the Stink House smelled like the bathroom did after Kevin had been in there with his comic books. Sometimes the stench lingered all the way down to the James's front porch. Other days, we barely noticed a stench at all.

For years, we watched with envy as my older brothers scaled the wall of the Stink House and taunted us from the roof, and sometimes even jumped off. Until we were 12, we didn't have the courage to climb up. Every few feet, randomly, a brick stuck out from the others just enough to offer a toe-stand, but to us as grade schoolers, the wall felt tall. During spring break of sixth grade, we finally challenged ourselves to pretend we were ninjas and climbed to the top. Ever since, the Stink House roof had become our meeting place and hangout.

"Tommy James, I double dog dare you to jump!" Kevin nodded below, looking Tommy right in the eye. Tommy started chewing his fingernails, and then tugging at his hair.

We knew this particular dare was coming. My brother Andrew had been the first in the neighborhood, when he was 14. But, we had only been climbing up to the roof for a few months, so none of us had yet mustered the courage to actually make the first dare. Kevin, being fresh off house arrest and usually the first one to activate any dares, was ripe and ready for adventure.

We hadn't had a decent dare in really long time, much less a double dog dare. Most of our dares had been stupid stuff like eating bugs or riding our bikes no-hands-and-no-feet down the hill, which we had mastered years ago.

Our dare system had strict rules. We've even written them down and signed them with bloody thumb-prints last summer. Teddy kept the signed Dare Rules document in a shoebox under his bed. One such rule was that once the "daree" successfully completed the dare, the "darer" had to immediately perform the same dare. That way, we were careful not to dare something we wouldn't do ourselves. We even installed a contingency we called *paying up* which usually some form of servitude.

"Gentlemen," I said, in my best Howard Cosell voice, "we officially have our first dare of the summer." I held my fist in front of my mouth as if I had a microphone.

"Tommy James, you have been challenged to jump off the Stink House roof. What are your pay-up stakes?" I moved the pretend microphone to Tommy's mouth.

"Lemme think," Tommy mumbled while tugging at his hair with one hand and chewing on the thumbnail of the other hand.

Kevin went into stare-down mode, boring his gaze into Tommy. Tommy sat down cross-legged and chewed on his left thumbnail while flicking pebbles with his right hand.

Murphy, Teddy's dog, a 15-pound mutt, started whining. Usually when we were on the Stink House roof Murphy would wait for us, content to sniff around the foundation of the building, the shrubs, and the fire hydrant. If we stayed too long, he would curl up and take a nap under a tree.

"Murph, go lie down," Teddy commanded, and Murphy dropped his head and tail, walked slowly to the shade of the shrubs, and lay down.

I felt that unzipping again, which was starting to become a familiar feeling. I knew that Kevin's dare scared the crap out of Tommy. I felt it in my unzipping as much as I heard it in Murphy's whine.

"Whaddya say, Tommy?" Kevin chided.

"I don't know," Tommy mumbled again. "You guys know I'm never any good at coming up with pay-up stakes." Tommy looked at his brother.

"Tommy, are you are you deferring your dare negotiations to Teddy?" I asked with the pretend microphone still in my hand. Tommy nodded.

"That's fair. Teddy, you're Switzerland. What're the stakes?" Kevin asked.

"Leave me out of this. I think the whole thing is a load of bull crap," Teddy said.

"Whaddya mean a load of bull crap?" Kevin said.

"We only just started coming up here this year," Teddy said, with that familiar and instant flash of darkness in his eyes, "Let's enjoy it for a while before one of us breaks a leg and our parents get all overprotective and shit."

"Tommy, you're right. Your brother is a massive buzzkill," Kevin argued. Teddy winced. He didn't like Kevin's insult of his brother.

"Fine, here's the deal," Teddy said, stepping up to defend his twin. "Kevin, you have two choices. One, you jump at the same time as Tommy, not after. Or two, if you don't jump, and Tommy gets hurt, you assume 100 percent full responsibility. If Tommy lands safely, you serve 100 percent servitude for exactly one month, thirty days, no questions asked." I knew that Teddy was stalling to give Tommy some time to get over his anxiety.

"What exactly does 'full responsibility' mean?" Kevin always wanted to be completely clear on what he was expected to do so that when he reneged on his end of the deal, which he always did, he could figure out some kind of loophole to crawl through. We all knew that one day he would make an excellent lawyer. I didn't want to argue, and I suspected Kevin was stalling too. I just wanted the dare to be real.

"It means that if Tommy gets hurt, you take full responsibility for any and all parental inquiries," Teddy clarified.

"So in other words, I take full blame?"

"Yep." Teddy nodded.

"So, I tell all parents that I pushed him, or what?"

"Yep," Teddy agreed again.

"I think 30 days servitude is a little excessive."

"Well, if the parents all think you pushed Tommy, you're likely to be grounded for most of that thirty days anyway," Teddy reasoned.

"Drop it to 75 percent, and I'm game."

75 percent servitude meant that Kevin would do whatever Tommy said for 30 days, but one out of every four times he had the right to refuse.

"Tommy James, Kevin Tomkins has dared you to jump off the Stink House roof. Kevin, Tommy has offered pay-up stakes as follows: If Tommy jumps and you don't, and he gets hurt, you will assume 100 percent responsibility, claiming to all parents that you pushed him. If Tommy jumps and he doesn't get hurt, you will serve 75 percent servitude to Tommy for a period of 30 days. Do you both accept these terms?" I laid out the rules, holding out my fist, initiating our signature dare swear.

"Hellz Yeahz! I'm fresh off a week of house arrest," Kevin boasted, stacking his fist on top of mine.

"Let's fucking DO THIS," Teddy said, putting his fist on top of Kevin's.

Murphy started barking.

"Tommy James, do you accept?" I asked.

"It's ON." Tommy sealed the dare swear with his open palm on top of our fists.

Murphy barked some more.

Tommy walked slowly to the edge of the roof.

Murphy continued barking.

"Jump or surrender to pay up!" Kevin taunted.

"You jump!" I called Kevin's bluff, nudging him with my elbow.

"That's a clear violation of the rules. Bystanders cannot interfere with a dare negotiation in any way," Kevin insisted without moving a muscle in his face, eyes wide open.

"I'm not a bystander, I'm the dare master."

"Yeah, but that doesn't mean you can make up new rules," Kevin argued. "Tommy, you gonna jump or pay up?"

Murphy jumped up and barked, wiggling his whole body.

"It's okay, boy. We'll be right down," Teddy said, and then turned to Tommy. "You don't gotta do anything you don't wanna do, Bro."

Tommy chewed his thumbnail and stared over the edge. Kevin paced behind him.

I looked over the edge.

I unzipped.

Buried in the leaves of the shrub below I saw the deflated remains of a purple balloon. It was hidden in plain view. *We Are the World* rang inside my head.

"Fuck the damn rules! I have a Wendell legacy to uphold!" I said, then took a deep breath and jumped. I didn't even give Kevin or Tommy warning so that they could jump with me.

I just jumped.

For a split moment I was weightless. It was one of those stand-still moments of life that I will never forget. Not because of what happened, but more because of how I felt. I must have held my breath the whole flight, because I felt like time stood still. The fall was definitely not any height that would be fatal, but enough to give me a mid-flight moment to contemplate my own death, and it wasn't at all scary.

Well, maybe just a little bit.

He hovered over me.

The Shadow.

Am I dead?

No. But this is kind of what death feels like. Weightless.

A half grin on his face, his hood covering most of his left eye.

For that moment, I felt both scared and comforted.

And as quickly as he was there, he was gone.

When I opened my eyes again, I found myself sitting inside an evergreen shrub. It was tall enough that I had to climb down to get to solid ground. Instinctively, I had somehow known not to try to land on my feet. What I didn't take into account was the branch factor. I was pretty beat up with bruises and scratches, nothing bad enough to require any kind of serious medical attention. But, I did have a rather large gash in my left calf.

"What the FUCK, Alex?" Kevin yelled.

"Upholding the Wendell legacy!" I hollered, proudly.

"You okay?" Teddy called down.

"Yeah. I'm fine. It's not that bad." I held my calf, blood dripping down to my ankle.

"That's badass," Teddy said, smiling down at me proudly.

"I think you both owe me servitude," I said once I wriggled myself to the ground and started brushing myself off.

"No fair, you didn't give us warning to jump along with you."

"You wouldn't have jumped anyway."

"I would too."

"You were negotiating servitude like it was your plan all along," Teddy pointed out.

"Neither of them was gonna jump," I said.

"I was just working up the nerve," Tommy said.

"I was waiting for Tommy," Kevin said.

"Then, why are you both still up there, and I'm down here?"

Then Teddy sat down on the edge and then turned himself around. Holding the edge, he dangled himself from the end and then let himself drop. Catlike, he landed softly on his feet. I'd never seen him do that before, but somehow I knew, he'd done it before, and more than once.

"Dammit, Alex, you're not okay. You're bleeding," he said.

"I'm fine," I insisted, pushing the hair out of my face.

"So fine that you don't even know you have a balloon stuck in your hair," he said, pulling the deflated purple balloon and its string from my hair and handing it to me. I shoved it into my pocket. A souvenir.

"Now, let me see your leg," he said.

He had a look in his eye, a sort of fascination with my wound. I thought maybe one day he might be a surgeon like his dad. The sight of blood certainly didn't bother him.

"It's nothing, really," I said.

"Alex, we gotta clean this up, or it'll get infected."

"Okay, Mrs. James," I said sarcastically.

As much as I protested, there were times that my friends insisted on treating me like a girl. They called it chivalry. I called it annoying. This time, as Teddy cupped my bleeding calf between his hands, I didn't mind. I kinda liked the attention, but only because it was from Teddy.

CHAPTER FIVE

Heart Dissection

Our little posse trampled onto the front porch of the James's house and deposited me in the rocking chair. The moms of our cul de sac neighborhood practiced the adage "It takes a village to raise a child." As kids, we knew which mom to go to for what need.

Mrs. James was our nurse, treating all cuts and scrapes, owies, and boo-boos. She didn't just have a first aid kit, she had a first aid CABINET.

Teddy was accident prone. Over the years, he'd broken his left ankle, his right wrist, more toes than we could remember, not to mention all the random skinned knees or sprained ankles. Mrs. James had good reason for maintaining her large stash of bandages, splints, slings, ace bandages and braces.

That day, the James's front door was closed with a note taped to the window.

Teddy & Tommy,
Had to run an errand.
Mrs. Tomkins is in charge.
Love & Kisses,
Mom

Tommy refolded the note on its worn edges and slid it through the mail slot.

"Shit-damn-fuck-a-fucking-duck," Kevin whined as he paced the front porch, "We *cannot* go to my house, my mom'll have a hissy fit over this. I just got off house arrest. I don't wanna spend the rest of today inside too."

"I guess 100 percent responsibility is out of the window," Teddy said sarcastically.

"Suits me. I'm happy to have Kevin as my servant for the next 30 days," I said.

"I dared Tommy, not you, Alex. All pay ups are null and void," Kevin said.

"Damn, Kevin, if you don't find a loophole, you fabricate one. I hope you go to law school when you grow up," I suggested.

"How do you think I get out of house arrest early every single time? I've got mad negotiation skills."

"Either that, or you're just annoying and your mom wants to get you outta the house," I chided.

"Seriously though, we can't go to my house. We just can't," Kevin pleaded. "Why does your dad insist on keeping the doors locked anyway? No one else in the neighborhood locks their doors, ever."

"We don't ask questions of Father, ever," Tommy said matter-of-factly.

"I'm fine, really. See, the bleeding's almost stopped."

"Shut up, Alex, and let us clean you up," Teddy said, reaching his hands between a crack in the floorboards.

"We have entry!" Teddy announced, holding up a key attached to a string.

"Where'd that come from?" Tommy asked.

"Mom told me she hid it here last month, after that time Father *accidentally* locked her out," Teddy answered.

"Oh. Yeah . . . ." Tommy said, looking off into the distance for a moment.

"Don't any of you ever tell anyone you know it's here." Teddy stopped, looking each of us in the eye. "Mom and I have a deal, I can use the key if, and only if, we make it look like we never did," Teddy said as he unlocked the door. "We can go in, but we have to clean everything up and leave the house like we were never here. Comprendé?" he said as he returned the key to its hiding place. "I mean it." Teddy held one hand on the door knob, blocking our entrance.

"Pinky swear." He held up his pinky finger.

One by one, we latched our pinkies to his and said, "I solemnly swear to keep this secret forever."

"SWEET!" Kevin gasped, relieved, as we made our way to the main bathroom.

Tommy dug through the first-aid cabinet while Kevin rummaged through the cupboard under the sink, throwing tampons at me. I sat down in the tub, throwing my legs over the side, and Teddy kneeled over my leg to inspect my wound. The blood was mostly dry, already starting to scab.

"It's fine, really," I protested as Teddy unwrapped one of the tampons and used it to dab at my wound.

He held my leg with such tenderness, one hand on the back of my calf, the other hand gently cleaning the wound. Tommy handed him a bottle of hydrogen peroxide. Teddy kept his hand on the back of my calf as he carefully set the cap of the peroxide on the edge of the tub and started pouring into it.

"Look what I found!" Kevin shouted, as he sprung out of the cupboard like a pogo stick. A dead grey mouse still in a trap dangled from his fingers.

Kevin bumped into Teddy, who then spilled the peroxide on my leg, far more than I needed. The wound foamed and fizzed.

"OUCH!" I screamed, and kicked in a knee-jerk reaction.

"Dammit, Kevin!" Teddy said, "Alex, are you okay?"

"I'm fine. Are you okay? I didn't mean to kick you. Reflex."

Kevin swung the dead mouse in front of Tommy's face. It was only a couple inches long and kinda cute, with soft, grey fur.

"Dude, is that really necessary?" Tommy said, pushing Kevin's arm away.

"Bro, Mom asked you to check that trap last night," Teddy scolded Tommy.

"I forgot."

"Well, it's done now. You can tell your mom she owes me one," Kevin said, setting to the task of extracting the dead mouse from the trap.

Teddy sat down on the floor in front of my leg. He put a dab of antiseptic ointment on the tip of a fresh tampon and dabbed at my now-clean wound until it had a nice layer of greasy goo. For a moment, I forgot that Tommy and Kevin were still in the room.

He's so gentle.

He opened a bandage and carefully sealed all its adhesive sides around the edges of my wound, running his fingers along the edges several times, so softly that it wasn't even enough pressure to really do much of anything.

And I liked it.

More than I wanted to admit.

My heart skipped a beat, several of them, actually. I felt a hiccup stuck in my chest.

"Let's dissect it!" Kevin suggested, using a demented, throaty voice.

"We've got supplies!" Tommy announced, producing two sets of cuticle scissors, two different sizes of tweezers, fingernail and toenail clippers, as well as bandage scissors, a couple of razor blades, and four pairs of latex gloves. Teddy pulled on a pair of latex gloves, snapping them at his wrists before he carefully placed the dead mouse belly-up in the center of the bathtub.

"What if your mom wants to use those tweezers to pluck her eyebrows again?" I asked, feeling just a tad sick to my stomach at the thought.

"She won't," Tommy said matter-of-factly. "She has a grooming kit in her master bath for that."

"But if it makes you feel better," Teddy added, "I'll sterilize these when I'm done."

"How are you gonna do that when you spilled all the peroxide on my leg?"

"I didn't spill all of it," he said, shaking the half-full bottle at me. "Besides, that's on Kevin."

"How 'bout you just toss 'em? I don't want those mouse-gut tweezers digging some splinter out of my finger someday."

"Fine. I'll toss 'em," he said, looking up at me with that softness in his eyes that brought made the stuck hiccup grow bigger.

Then, he looked down at the mouse. The look on his face changed to a focused fascination. The tip of his tongue peeked out of the corner of his mouth. Teddy used the razor blade to begin the first cut just under the critter's jaw, and then carefully snipped the furry skin with the cuticle scissors bit by bit until there was a long incision running from its jaw to its tail.

I unzipped.

And for a moment time stopped, like the weightlessness of my fall from the Stink House.

As I studied Teddy's expression, his face aged. I couldn't tell if I was looking at an age-progression of Teddy, or a superimposition of his father, the determined surgeon, preparing for a procedure.

"EWWW! Gross!" Tommy's screech snapped me back.

"Dude, that's cool!" Kevin said lunging toward the mouse.

"Back off!" Teddy said without looking up, focusing his gaze on the tweezers carefully grasping the skin at the incision. Using the cuticle scissors and the tweezers, he craftily peeled the pelt away from the body. He seemed to know what he was doing.

He looked curious, and at the same time grown-up.

My thoughts about Teddy swirled around in my head, matching the shivers in my unzipped spine and the flutters in my stomach. I closed my eyes and shook my head, trying to convince myself that

I was just dizzy from the pain of peroxide on my wound. This was Teddy, just Teddy.

Holy Shit!

Do I like LIKE Teddy?

No way..

Maybe?

I think I do.

Oh SHIT!

"Get a Dixie cup, and fill it with water. We'll use it to irrigate the incision," Teddy instructed.

I played along, pretending I was one of the scrub nurses on *St. Elsewhere*.

"What's with all the technical terms?" I asked while drizzling the water over the mouse.

"We gotta make it real."

I like following his lead.

Teddy pulled the furry skin away from the incision, revealing all the glories of dissection. It was a little too much for Tommy, though. He gagged, tilted his head into the sink, took a swig of water straight from the faucet, swished it in his mouth, and spit it back out like a boxer. Then he sat down on the toilet seat, putting his head between his knees.

In the meantime, Teddy had surgically removed the internal organs from the mouse and was spreading them out on a gauze pad.

"You gotta see this!" Teddy said, as he got up out of the tub and placed the gauze pad on the bathroom counter, nodding at me. While Tommy stayed a safe distance away on the toilet seat, Kevin took advantage of the empty tub and started digging at the remains of the mouse corpse in the tub. I leaned over the counter with Teddy as he gently used the tweezers to pull the organs apart from each other.

"I think this is the liver," he said, using the cuticle scissors to cut the deep brown-red, silky-looking flaps away from the rest.

"And obviously, the intestines," he said pulling the spaghetti mess away from the rest.

"Oh my God!" he said, rolling a tiny, red, oddly shaped ball to a clear patch of the gauze pad.

"It's the heart!" he said in an excited whisper.

"It's so tiny," I said.

"I wish I could see how it works from the inside. I wanna know how the heart works," Teddy said as he mimicked the pumping of the heart with the pulse of his tweezers.

Yup, I definitely like LIKE Teddy.

Gulp.

"That's demented," Kevin said as he grabbed the cuticle scissors out of Teddy's hand, climbed back into the bathtub and stabbed the mouse in the neck. Kevin's approach was far less precise, more grotesque, and frankly, more what one might expect from an almost-13-year-old boy. Holding it in place with the stake of the cuticle scissors, he started sawing its head off with a razor blade. After several saws, the head still wasn't completely severed. He gave up and used the toenail clippers to snap off each of the legs and its tail.

"Oh, as if what you are doing isn't demented at all?" Teddy said, annoyed that Kevin had destroyed his careful precision.

Then we heard footsteps on the stairs. Mrs. James was home from running errands.

"Teddy? Tommy? What are you boys doing in there? You had better not be filling the bathtub with toads from the creek again!"

The doorknob to the bathroom jiggled, but thankfully, Teddy locked it.

"No Mom, Alex scraped up her leg. We're just cleaning her up."

"Is she okay? Let me in, and I'll take a look."

"I'm fine, Mrs. James. It's just a little scrape."

"Okay, make sure you put some antiseptic ointment on it. And please make sure you leave the bathroom as you found it. You know how your father is about sterilization."

"Will do," Teddy said, catching his brother's eye in a knowing look. The level of clean Mr. James demanded was more than sanitary. Being a surgeon, he required operating-room sterilization of all kitchen and bathroom surfaces. As a result, the James's house almost always smelled of ammonia. Mrs. James spent the better part of her day making sure it stayed that way.

"Are you kids hungry?" Mrs. James asked.

"Hellz yeah!" Kevin shouted as he burst out of the bathroom, following Mrs. James down the stairs, Tommy close behind him. When it came to cleaning up, Kevin always found a way to disappear. We learned long ago that it was best to let him leave, because he had a tendency to make more messes while we were trying to clean.

Teddy threw me a half smile as he picked up the bloody tweezers Kevin had dropped on the floor and added them to the sink he was filling with hot water and bleach. Then, he sat down in the bathtub once again. He laid the mouse carcass out flat, trying his best to piece it back together. I stood by the bathroom counter and watched as he seemed to forget I was there. He had a sad, yet rather peaceful look on his face.

No.

Sad isn't the word.

Sorrow.

Teddy looked sorrowful.

His face was long. His eyelids were all but closed, looking down, his hands cupped around the mouse. I stood there watching him. I couldn't tell for sure, but I thought maybe he was crying. Then, he looked up, right in my eyes.

I unzipped again.

Oddly, I was the one startled. That moment, that look—I felt it wedge itself into a special memory receptacle of my brain. I knew at the time that this conversation was one of those never-forget-easy-to-access-memory-moments that I would cherish.

"Alex, do you think animals have souls?" he asked.

I sat down on the edge of the tub next to him. A subtle heaviness filled the bottom tip of my heart and seemed to anchor into the center of my diaphragm, making my breath dense.

"Yeah. I think they do."

"I think so too," he said, looking right into my eyes. He had both a faraway look and a penetrating stare. There was a long, awkward moment.

Then he broke the silence as his faraway look turned into a happy-go-lucky-playful smile.

"Maybe this mouse died just so we could dissect it today," Teddy said as he bounced out of the tub and took the mouse to the toilet.

"Yea, though I walk through the valley of the shadow of death. Ashes to ashes. Dust to dust. Now we lay you, Jerry-Mouse, to rest. We are grateful to you for sacrificing yourself for us in the name of science and adventure. Go forth into the spirit world where you may serve a deeper purpose. May you now nibble happily away on a big chunk of Swiss cheese in mouse heaven. We will remember you always."

He dropped the mouse carcass into the toilet, took a deep breath, and closed his eyes. Then, he leaned down over the toilet and let a slow, lingering, drop of spit dribble out of his mouth onto the mouse. It all seemed so peaceful, so complete, and yet so very odd. Just odd.

Teri Leigh

CHAPTER SIX

The Tree Fort

Deeper into the woods in our backyards stood a large oak tree where my brothers had started building a tree fort years ago. Six two-by-fours nailed to the trunk served as a makeshift ladder. The tree fort itself was just a large platform nestled into the branches.

We'd run by and played around this tree our whole lives, but never took the time to really look at it, much less admire its presence. The tree was huge, massively huge. It was a grandmother of a tree, well over a hundred years old, and probably mother to most of the trees in its vicinity. The lowest branch was a good 15 feet off the ground, higher than the roof of the Stink House. The platform, which was the size of a small bedroom, sat in the heart of the tree just above that first branch, resting on several branches.

Our neighbor, Freaky Mr. Weismann, who used to own a construction company, had worked with my brothers to secure it. The boards nailed to the trunk were spaced too far apart to be a real ladder, but clearly a start to one. I remember them teasing me when I was younger that they did that on purpose to keep the riff-raff out —namely, me and my friends.

"Ta-Da!" Teddy hollered from the top rung of the ladder, pulling his arm out from elbow-deep in a knotty hole of the tree. Dangling from his fingers was a key ring with a single padlock key attached. He fit the key into the padlock on the trap door entrance to the fort.

"Can you believe that we never thought to look there for the key?" Teddy laughed.

"When did you find this?" I asked.

"Yesterday morning after my paper route, during my walk with Murphy," he said, but I knew he was lying. He'd been up there before, probably many times.

"You go first." Kevin elbowed Tommy. "This is your chance for Stink House jump redemption!"

Tommy walked to the base of the tree and looked up at Teddy.

"Climbing *up* is much easier than jumping down," Teddy said as Tommy stepped onto the first rung of the ladder.

"I'll be right behind you," I suggested.

Tommy stepped both feet onto the first rung.

"There's a big knot midway between the first and second rungs. Put your left foot there," Teddy guided. Tommy was visibly nervous, anxious, but Teddy's calm guidance from above seemed to steady him.

"Now grab the second rung with your right hand." Tommy followed Teddy's instruction, slowly, overly cautious. "Push all your weight into your left foot and pull yourself up so you can lift your right leg to the second rung."

"You've got this," I assured.

"See that large hole above the second rung? Grab it with your left hand, and getting both your feet on the second rung is easy."

Teddy talked Tommy up to the third and fourth rungs with the same precise directions. I followed in suit. When Tommy got both his feet on the fourth rung, I stood firmly on the second rung with Kevin below me on the first rung.

"Be careful, the next rung is loose," Teddy warned, and Tommy's whole body tightened.

I unzipped.

A sharp chill shivered down my spine, originating from a tiny hole in the zipper between my shoulder blades. Out of nowhere, I felt a quivering on my insides, and my blood started running like a heavily trafficked highway. But I also got this heavy rock in the pit of my stomach. My body felt both paralyzed by the heavy rock, yet overly fidgety from the quivering on my insides. The feelings, purely physical, came out of nowhere.

"You got this, Bro," Teddy encouraged, and his voice silenced the temporary chaos I had felt.

"SHIT!" Tommy screamed when he lost his grip on the knot he was holding with his left hand. At the same time, his right foot slipped on the loose rung. Although his left foot was firmly planted, his right foot kept slipping.

"I'M COMING DOWN! I'M COMING DOWN!" he hollered and started to lower his foot right towards my head.

"Kevin, you gotta move!" I screamed, trying to lower myself to give space for Tommy.

"The point is to go up the ladder, not down, you idiots," Kevin chided.

"Tommy, stop! You're gonna step on my head!" I hollered.

"I CAN'T! I GOTTA COME DOWN!" He was genuinely scared.

I'd never seen such a look in Tommy's eyes as he stared at me from above.

"Just climb the friggin' ladder, Tommy," Kevin yelled.

"I can't," Tommy said. This time his voice was barely a whisper.

Tommy lowered his foot, and I quickly moved my hand to leave room for it, but he still pinched my pinky finger slightly with his big toe. When I looked up, he was hugging the tree trunk for dear life, with both arms wrapped around the tree like a toddler hanging on his mother's neck.

"Tommy, come on up. It's so worth it. I promise," Teddy coaxed from above.

"I'm not movin'," Tommy insisted.

I looked up at Teddy, lost for what to do.

Teddy shook his head.

And then I felt afraid too.

My shaky paralysis consumed my entire body and took over my mood as well. It started with the pain in my pinky finger where Tommy's foot had pinched me, and that screeching feeling grew through my hand, my arm, and eventually my torso. I felt the shaking on my insides. I knew if I let go of the tree, my hands would shake like an old woman with Parkinson's. To stop my shaking, I closed my eyes for a moment and held the tree in a tight bear hug.

Move him.

The Shadow's chilling voice breathed into my right ear.

How?

When I opened my eyes again, before they fully focused, I saw him straddling a high branch.

You know how. Use your will.

I closed my eyes again and took a deep breath. My back zipped up, sealing itself closed securely. Something moved in me, like my stomach was growling, but not. The shakiness shifted from a paralyzing anxiety into a forceful drive.

"It's steady now, Tommy," I said, putting my left hand back on the loose rung, making sure it didn't move.

"I've got you," I said, grabbing his right foot and guiding it to secure on the knot just below the loose rung.

"KEVIN, MOVE!" I didn't recognize my own voice; it was deeper, more authoritative. It rose up from the pit of my belly and vibrated with a confidence in my core I'd never felt before.

It worked.

Kevin pushed himself away from the tree and leapt to the ground. He picked up a stick and started singing to himself as he circled around the bottom of the tree waiting for us.

"Do your balls hang low? Do they wobble to and fro?
Can you tie 'em in a knot? Can you tie 'em in a bow?
Can you swing 'em over your shoulder
Like a continental soldier?
Do your nuggies haaaaang looooooow????"

I guided Tommy, step-by-step, my hands showing his feet where to go, my voice coaching him safely to the ground.

"Thanks, Alex," Teddy said. I had been so focused on Tommy that I hadn't noticed that Teddy had climbed down behind us.

"No problem."

"You okay, Bro?" Teddy asked, his hand on Tommy's shoulder as Tommy sat on a large tree root, arms folded over his belly.

"I don't want to talk about it," he said.

"We just wanna make sure you're okay," I said.

"I don't want to talk about it," Tommy said, more forcefully, as he pushed Teddy's hand off his shoulder and stood up. He grabbed a stick and followed Kevin, singing along.

"Ohhhh, she burped and she farted and she spit on the floor
And the blast from her ass blew the door knob off the door."

Convinced that Tommy would be fine, Teddy climbed back up the tree, motioning for me to join him. When we got to the top, Teddy sat on the edge of the tree fort platform, dangling his legs over the side, watching Kevin and Tommy down below. But I felt woozy. We were so high up, and there were no walls or railings.

"It's perfectly safe," Teddy said, patting a spot next to him.

I sheepishly got down on all fours and crawled over to him.

"I did that the first time too," he admitted, looking me straight in the eye. A whole silent conversation occurred between us before I found my tongue again.

"Why the hell didn't you tell us?"

"You know better than to ask me that."

"I wish you would've told ME."

"You couldn't keep a secret this big."

"Yeah, I suppose you're right about that."

"You needed this one to yourself for a while, didn't you?"

"Yeah, I did."

"How many times have you been up here?" Sound finally came out of my mouth.

"I don't know. A lot."

"When did you first come up here?"

"Some time last summer, I guess. I come up here every morning after my paper route."

Murphy whined up at us, his top feet on the first rung of the ladder, trying to climb up too.

"No boy, you can't come up here today," Teddy said to Murphy, "but you can go lie down in your hole and wait for me."

Teddy always spoke to Murphy like he was another human being, in complete sentences, and Murphy always did exactly as Teddy asked.

"How come you never tried to bring us up here before?"

"I guess I thought of it as my secret place."

"What do you do when you're up here?"

"I don't know. I think about life. Sometimes I write."

Teddy and I had writing in common. He wrote song lyrics, and I wrote short stories. But we rarely ever talked about our writing, and never ever shared our writing with each other.

"Why did you decide to bring us up here now?"

"It just felt like it was time," he said, leaning over his legs to look down at Kevin and Tommy, balancing on a lightning-struck dead branch, still singing while swinging sticks around like swords.

> *"And the old man hit her with a bucket full of shit*
> *And the moon shined brightly on the nipple of her tit."*

"Too soon, I guess." He winked at me.

"Yeah, I suppose so."

"I never noticed that before." Teddy pointed down at a sharp dagger of a branch from the dead side of the tree about eight inches in diameter. It was almost straight down from the corner of the platform where we sat, and it looked like a giant sabre pointing straight out of the ground.

"Excalibur," I said.

"Excalibur." Teddy said, smiling. "I like it."

Kevin and Tommy, still singing their stupid song, circled it without even noticing it was a giant stalagmite.

"Guys, look up. See that? It's a giant sword," Teddy pointed.

"COOL!" Kevin said.

"Alex named it Excalibur."

"Super COOL!" Tommy said.

"Are you two gonna stay up there all day?" Kevin asked.

"I wouldn't mind staying all day," I said.

"Well you're gonna have to come down sometime," Tommy said. I heard a hint of jealousy in his voice. Teddy heard it too.

Teddy was on the ground before I even thought to get up from my seat over the edge. As I leaned over my legs to see my friends below I gasped. If I just kept leaning until I lost my seat, I would impale myself right on Excalibur.

And as quickly as I had that thought looking down, the zipper in my back split wide open, and a zinging sensation sent shivers through my spine. It startled me so much that I leaned back, so far that I fell over on my back.

Gazing up through the upper branches of the mighty oak, I saw a long, white string up near the top attached to a half deflated purple balloon.

CHAPTER SEVEN

The Joint

"You're looking particularly grubby today, Sis. What have you and your friends been up to?" Dave asked, shoveling taco meat into three empty shells.

"Thanks, I think?" I took the taco he offered and sat at my place at the table.

"You're welcome," Dave said, looking me right in the eye and smiling. I didn't entirely trust it.

"Why are you smiling like that?" I asked.

"We just want to know what you've been up to," Andrew said.

My entire life I had been the kid sister bullied by twin brothers eight years my senior. I was their punching bag, their dog toy, their squeaker. They had never gone out of their way to do anything nice for me. They usually ignored me entirely. But when they did notice me, they treated me like an annoying gnat they swatted away. On the rare occasion they did take interest in me, I couldn't help but be suspicious.

"Since when do you give a crap about what I'm up to?"

"Language!" Mom said to me with that automatic-disapproving-mom tone.

"You can tell us," Andrew said. "We won't hassle you."

"I don't believe you."

"C'mon, Sis. We haven't hassled you once since we moved into the loft above the garage," Dave added.

"We're over all that sibling taunting bullshit."

"Language!" Mom said again.

"Alex, the boys have a point, you do look a little more grubby than usual. We'd all like to know what you and your friends were up to today," Dad prodded.

"We went up in your old tree fort today," I squeaked.

"Shit!" Andrew blurted out, and a diced tomato spewed across the table. Dave swallowed and looked up at me in a tiny moment of shock.

"Language!" Mom said, "I am going to start charging for a swear jar."

"Sorry, Mom."

"How did you get in?" Andrew asked.

"Teddy found the key in the hollow of the tree."

"Well then, isn't Teddy the smart one," Dave said.

"Did you go up?" Andrew asked.

"Teddy and I climbed up, but Tommy and Kevin stayed down." I said, "It's not exactly easy to get up there."

"Yeah, it probably needs a couple more ladder rungs," Dave said.

"And some walls," Andrew added.

"And a roof," Dave suggested.

"How come you never finished it?" I asked.

"When Mr. Weismann said we had to start paying him, we just quit." Andrew added.

"Yeah, Mr. Weismann had this vision of it being really solid, home construction quality, only up in the tree," Dave said.

"He drew up plans and everything. We were gonna put in insulation, and real windows, built-in bunkbeds, and a skylight," Andrew reminisced.

"No wonder he wanted you to pay him," Dad said.

"It would've been a cool-ass tree fort," Dave said, a dazed look in his eye. Then he looked up, a dead stare at Andrew.

"Are you thinking what I'm thinking?" Dave asked Andrew with a glint in his eye.

"Dude! We've gotta finish it!" Andrew said.

"We've got a lot more construction experience under our belts now. We don't need Weismann anymore," Dave said.

"I'd bet our boss will give us a discount, so it won't cost much!" Andrew suggested.

"Wait! What?" I stopped in my tracks on my way to get another taco. "What do you need a tree fort for now? You've got the garage loft. You said yourself that you haven't been up there in years," I said.

"Your sister is right, boys. You abandoned that fort years ago. You have school and work and the garage loft. Let her have the tree fort. Every kid her age should have a decent tree fort," Dad said, while Mom gave them both a disapproving mom-look.

"I'm not sure that thing is safe for those kids as it is," Mom said. "You shouldn't be going up there, Alex."

"Precisely why we should finish it," Dave said.

Dad stood up, pulled out his wallet and slapped $50 in the center of the table.

"For Alex's birthday. You boys understand that if you take this money, you relinquish any ownership rights to her."

"We could do it up real nice and take pictures for a brochure, and then maybe people will hire us to build more," Dave said, looking at Andrew. "It'd be a prototype!"

"Deal," Andrew said, offering his hand to Dad to seal the deal. Dave stood up and offered his hand to Dad as well.

"If I smell even the tiniest whiff of you hassling Alex about this, or not respecting her ownership, I will terminate your lease on the garage loft."

"Yes, sir," the twins said in unity.

"And you can get it done by her birthday?" Dad said, his hand still holding the money.

"Yes, sir," the twins said in unity, again.

"Alex, you understand that you and your friends are not to go near the tree fort, much less up into it, until your brothers have finished construction?"

"Yes, sir," I said, mimicking my brothers.

"Happy birthday, Alex. It looks like you got yourself a tree fort," Dad said, tugging on the end of my braid.

The next morning, I met my friends at the Stink House and we walked to the base of Excalibur where told them what my brothers had offered.

"You know that they are gonna be assholes about it and want access anytime they want," Tommy said.

"Yeah, they'll just kick us out at their whim," Kevin agreed.

"I don't think so. Dad made them shake on it. It's my birthday present. If they hassle us, Dad's gonna kick 'em out of the loft."

"Might I remind you, Alex," Dave's voice startled us from above, "your part in the deal is that you and your rugrat friends stay away until construction is complete." He spoke in a squeaky voice, letting as little air out of his lungs as possible as he passed the joint to Andrew.

"I didn't know you guys smoked," I said.

"And if you want this tree fort finished, you're not gonna tell, either," Dave added as they scurried down to meet us, a scrappy spiral notebook in hand.

"You think I give a shit if Mom and Dad find out that I smoke?" Andrew said, playing it off as if the joint were a regular cigarette.

"I know that's not a cigarette, you dumbass," I said, staring at Andrew.

"You want a hit, Sissy?" Andrew held the joint out to me.

"Bro! So not cool!" Dave said, taking the joint from Andrew.

"She's gonna try it sometime. Might as well be with us," Andrew said.

"No thanks. I'm good," I said.

"Ding ding ding. Right answer," Dave said.

"I'll take a hit," Kevin said with a heavy breath.

"Chunk speaks," Andrew said.

Kevin grabbed the sides of his belly and shook them vigorously.

"Dude, nice truffle shuffle!" Andrew laughed, patting Kevin's chubby belly.

"So are ya gonna let me have a hit or not?" Kevin asked.

"This isn't like swallowing gulps of chocolate syrup," Dave said snuffing out the joint and stashing it in an Altoids tin that he shoved in his back pocket.

"Whatever, that's lame," Kevin rolled his eyes.

Dave and Andrew sat down with us on a couple of logs and started showing us their sketched-out building plans. They'd even written out a complete list of materials, including a list of tools they needed to borrow from Mr. Weismann.

"We thought this third of the platform could be a front porch, with no roof, so you could gaze up at the stars at night," Dave said.

"And we'd build a door here, and windows on each side of the enclosed space, with a skylight, and built-in bunkbeds!" Andrew announced.

"How long is this gonna take?" I asked.

"If we work evenings and weekends, we could get it done by Halloween," Andrew projected.

"Halloween?!" I argued. "No way. Dad said it's for my birthday!"

"Do you want it done fast, or do you want it done right?" Andrew asked.

After a rather intense negotiation we agreed that they would finish a basic structure with a front porch and one window by my birthday, and they could work on the skylight and built-in bunk beds later.

"We will officially hand over the keys to the Joint on Alex's birthday," Andrew added, using his fingers to emphasize the air-quotes of "the Joint."

"Shake on it," Teddy said, standing up, holding out his fist between us. All six of us piled our hands in one huge fist, officially christening the big tree fort as the Joint.

CHAPTER EIGHT

Angry Man

A couple days later, I woke up at 5:30 am and couldn't get back to sleep. I waited in the big rocking chair on the James's front porch for Teddy to get back from his paper route, hoping he'd let me join him on his morning adventures. When Murphy saw me, he broke into a full sprint, leaping into my lap and nearly knocking the rocking chair over completely.

"Hi, Bud," I said to Murphy, scratching behind his ear.

"Hello," Teddy said as he stepped onto the porch, not looking at me directly. He wore a brace on his left wrist and had a fresh black eye.

"I couldn't sleep," my voice said. What I wanted to say was "*What happened to you this time?*"

"Oh," he said as he took off his paperboy smock and stashed it under the porch.

"Can I come with you?" I asked as Teddy strapped on his backpack.

"Sure. But we walk. We don't talk," he said firmly.

I had so many questions. I wanted to ask him what was wrong, what happened, and so much more. But his message was crystal clear.

Silence.

"Murph, come!" Teddy said, snapping his fingers by his left thigh. Murphy jumped off my lap and ran to Teddy, heeling at Teddy's left side.

I followed a few steps behind. When we got to the creek bed, he sat down on a large, flat rock and pulled a bag of dog treats out of his backpack. I sat down on a nearby rock.

"Sit." Murphy sat down and looked up at Teddy expectantly.

"Sneeze." Murphy shook his head and snorted like a sneeze.

"Shake." Murphy offered Teddy his paw.

"Other paw." Murphy switched paws.

"High five." Murphy lifted his paw higher and patted Teddy's waiting hand in the air.

"Down." Murphy lay down.

"Hide." Murphy covered his eyes with both his paws.

"Roll over." Murphy rolled over.

"Dead." Murphy rolled to his back and flipped his head back.

"Pogo." Murphy repeatedly jumped on his hind legs like he was on a pogo stick.

"Stop." Murphy sat down and looked up at Teddy, who finally offered him a couple treats and head scratches.

"Good boy." Then they repeated the entire montage of tricks, only this time without words, using only hand gestures. After Murphy got his second round of treats, Teddy turned his back to Murphy.

"Scratch," he said as he patted his back, and Murphy stood up on his hind legs, scratching Teddy's back with his front paws.

"That's a new one," I said, impressed.

Teddy just nodded at me, as if to remind me of my promise of silence. Then, he patted his shoulder, and Murphy stopped scratching and placed his chin on Teddy's shoulder, rewarded with a treat.

"Come." Teddy stood up, put his backpack on again, and started walking deeper into the woods, far beyond the Joint. I followed, again a few steps behind. Murphy stayed close, wandering just far enough to track down a scent, but always coming back with the slightest of whistle from Teddy.

Until he didn't.

We found him digging underneath a gnarly shrub, stubbornly intent at getting to whatever it was he smelled. Teddy stopped and gasped. He then positioned himself between me and the shrub so I couldn't see what Murphy was digging.

"MURPHY!" Teddy snapped, slapping his hand on his thigh. Murphy immediately scurried to Teddy's side, sitting down obediently at Teddy's left heel. Teddy pulled a leash out of his backpack and snapped it to Murphy's collar.

That's odd, Teddy almost never uses a leash with Murphy.

Teddy stood still, staring at the space where Murphy had started digging, holding Murphy's leash close and tight. When I caught up, I had to grab the trunk of a nearby tree to steady myself. What I saw knocked the wind out of me.

Covered lightly with dried leaves and brush were the lifeless bodies of three large dogs. They were Brandy, Whiskey, and

Bourbon, Mr. Mackey's hunting dogs, who lived at the other end of our street, by the Stink House. When they weren't hunting, which was most of the time, they ran freely through the neighborhood. Mr. Mackey, the neighborhood drunk, wasn't very good at taking care of them.

We stood and stared for a long time. Too long. Teddy eventually put his hand on my shoulder, nudging me to turn around. But it didn't feel like Teddy's hand at all. I unzipped. There was a shiver in my spine again, and a cold metallic zing zapped down my back.

For a half of a moment, barely a flash, Teddy wasn't Teddy.

He was the Shadow.

And then he was Teddy again.

He took my elbow in his protective grip, and we walked to the Stink House. The whole walk Teddy held Murphy's leash in one hand, and my elbow in his other hand. I didn't know if it was to protect me or to steady himself. Either way, I liked it. Once settled, our legs dangling over the edge of the Stink House roof, Teddy finally broke his silence.

"That was the scariest thing I've ever seen in my life."

I detected the sound of tears squeaking at the edge of his words.

"Are you okay?" I asked.

"No," he hesitated, staring down at the space between his legs, "—but I will be." He finished. "Are you okay?"

I nodded.

I felt suspended in the space of silence.

Unbearable silence.

"I noticed they hadn't been around the last few days," I said to break the silence. But when Teddy didn't reply, I wondered if I hadn't actually spoken at all, so I tried again. "I thought Mr. Mackey had probably gone on another hunting trip with them for the week."

"It's not hunting season," he said, matter-of-factly.

"Oh."

"Someone killed those dogs," he said flatly. "Viciously," he added in a half whisper.

Silence.

Teddy eyes flicked back and forth. But it was more than that, he was calculating his thoughts, adding together memories. He knew more than he was saying. He saw more than he was sharing.

"Who did that?" I asked again.

Teddy didn't answer. He just dropped his head, landing his gaze again at the gap between his legs. He began to breathe heavily. With each breath, his head lowered more, until eventually his head was in his hands between his knees. His fingers clawed at his hair, yanking and pulling as he shook his head and moaned.

I put my hand on his back, and he softened. But, at the same time that familiar spot between my shoulder blades stayed open. This time I felt like some monster had sliced my back-heart open with his Freddy Krueger razor fingernails and dug into my body, trying to shred my heart. I felt raw, exposed, vulnerable, and . . . well, terrified.

When I lifted my hand off Teddy's back the feeling softened, but Teddy tightened. I let my hand rest again and the feeling intensified, and Teddy softened. I ultimately decided it was better to hold Teddy and feel the pain myself than to see him hold it all himself. So, I pressed my flat palm into the space between his shoulder blades and held his elbow with my other hand.

And we sat there, silent but quivering—not a crying quiver, but more a cold shiver—for what felt like an hour, but was probably only a few minutes. My eyes wouldn't focus. I just stared down at the ground where Murphy laid in the shade, looking up at us. As much as I tried to ignore him, I couldn't.

The Shadow was there, calmly petting Murphy.

"I don't know," Teddy said, shaking his head in his hands. "I just don't know."

"What do you need?"

"Your hand there helps. Just don't move."

"Okay."

Suddenly, Teddy sat upright, straight. His eyes had a fierceness to them unlike anything I had ever seen before, not just in Teddy, but ever.

"I know who did this, and he wanted me to find them."

"Who?"

"The same guy who did this," he said, holding up his hand with the wrist brace and pointing to his black eye. He then rested his hand on his thigh, palm up, fingers open, inviting me to hold it. Holding hands wasn't something we had ever done before. But somehow, in that moment, it felt natural, like something we did normally. I let my fingers fold in between his.

"Angry Man," he whispered, squeezing my hand slightly harder than was comfortable.

When we were much younger, Teddy had recurring Angry Man nightmares. When we got old enough for campfire stories, he started making up Angry Man stories. Every story had a similar element: Angry Man would whisper horrible things in little boys' ears as they slept. It started as just insults, but then turned to threats. Scary, horrifying threats. Unabomber terroristic level threats. But we all just thought Angry Man was someone Teddy made up.

"What do you mean? Angry Man?"

"Alex, Angry Man isn't just a nightmare or a monster I made up for campfire stories. Angry Man is a real person, and you know who he is."

"Is Angry Man—?" I started to ask, but he interrupted me.

"Don't say it out loud," he said, pleading with his eyes.

The spot at the back of my heart throbbed, a deep ache that wouldn't quit. I felt my heart beating on my back. Teddy dropped my hand and let his head fall back into his hands between his knees. Instinctively, I rest my hand on his back again, this time prepared for the rawness.

"I poked the bear," he said with a muffled voice as he continued to shake his head in his hands. "I poked the bear, and now the bear is MAD."

CHAPTER NINE

Murphy

A couple days later, as the four of us were walking home from the corner store, Teddy called for Murphy. But, Murphy didn't come. We walked up the street, all calling for Murphy, but Murphy didn't come.

Then, Teddy took off running towards a lump in the middle of the road at the end of his driveway. Kevin, Tommy and I ran towards him, but stopped 10 feet short. My back unzipped all the way from the base of my skull down to my tailbone.

Day turned to grey.

Not night. Not light. Just grey.

Dense, heavy, fog-cloud grey.

Without a cloud in the sky.

The lump was Murphy.

Dead.

"I poked the bear, and now the bear is MAD."

CHAPTER TEN

The Shining

Our little neighborhood that once had four free-roaming dogs and four chattery, playful children, became quiet.

Silent.

Fresh-snow quiet.

In July.

I knocked on the James's door instead of ringing the doorbell. Something about my bare knuckles on the old wood felt better than the yellowed, plastic doorbell button. It was more natural. Raw. Like I felt.

Mrs. James opened the door, her sad eyes gazing down at me as she slowly shook her head, just as she had every day since Murphy died. Teddy wouldn't come out again today.

"You can come with me to Kevin's," Tommy said as he pushed by his mom and out the door.

"And become a video game zombie who actually drinks the new Coke like you? No, thank you."

"Suit yourself. Kevin's so lucky his dad could get a Nintendo at that trade show before it's available to the general public. Super Mario rocks!"

"Have fun!" I waved as Tommy trotted off towards Kevin's house.

"Please Alex, come by again. I think it means a lot to him that you try."

"I will. Thank you, Mrs. James."

She quietly shut the door behind her just as my mom beeped her car horn at me from our driveway, leaving for her part-time job at the public library.

"Wanna come with me?" she asked, rolling her window down.

"Sure."

"He'll come out again, just give him some time."

"I know."

"It's only been a week."

"I know."

A half hour later, I sat on the floor of the horror section of the library stacks, out of my mom's view. I ran my fingers across the line of worn paperback books, mostly with black covers. I pulled each one off the shelf, read the back cover, and organized them in piles for myself.

Yes. No. Maybe.

Carrie.
A girl gets bullied in school when she gets her first period.
No, thank you.

Christine.
A car possessed with supernatural forces.

Maybe.

Cujo.
A rabid St. Bernard.
No way.

The Dead Zone.
A guy comes out of a coma with psychic powers.
Hm.

Firestarter.
A girl starts fires with her mind.
Intriguing.

Pet Semetary.
Too soon.

Salem's Lot.
Vampires in Maine.
Nah.

The Shining.
A writer in a haunted hotel for the winter.
YES!

After re-alphabetizing the no's and maybe's back on the shelf, I stacked *Christine, The Dead Zone, Firestarter,* and *The Shining* in the crook of my elbow. I sat down in the cushy window seat of the library, out of view from the librarian's desk so Mom wouldn't hassle me about my reading choices. I started reading at 9:00 a.m. and didn't move until Mom came to get me when her shift was over at 1:00 p.m.

"Are you sure you want to be reading that?" she asked as we got in the car.

"It's really good!" I said.

"I know it is," she said, a glint in her eye.

"And," she paused, "it gave me really nasty nightmares."

"I can handle it," I said, mostly to get her to leave me alone, but also to reassure myself.

"I believe you."

"I was a little older than you the first time I read a grown-up horror book."

"What book was that?"

"*The Haunting of Hill House*, by Shirley Jackson."

"I'll have to add that one to my list."

"Come to think of it, I wonder if Stephen King was influenced by Jackson. *The Shining* and *Christine* have similar flavors."

"You've read *Christine*?" I asked, surprised.

She nodded.

"*Firestarter*?"

"Yup."

"*Pet Sematary*?"

"I've read all of Stephen King's books. He's a master at his craft. And given what just happened, I don't recommend you read *Pet Sematary* right now."

"No way."

"And I would suggest you wait until after you get your period before you read *Carrie*."

I blushed.

"I had no idea you liked horror."

"There's a lot you don't know about me." She smiled.

I felt a much-needed warmth coat my insides.

Mom was right about the nightmares. They started that very night. It was the same dream, several times in one night. I was in a bathroom, and when I closed the medicine cabinet the word REDRUM appeared on the fogged-up mirror. Then, a decaying old woman climbed out of the bathtub, and her lips looked like Mrs. Schmidt's, sewn shut. That's when I would wake up with that chilling feeling, the same feeling I had when Teddy said he poked the bear.

When the nightmares woke me, four separate times that night, I opened my journal. Over the course of the night, I filled six pages with "it's only a dream" repeated over and over again, written like a school-girl punishment assignment. That in itself was its own form of haunting.

The next day, I settled in the same window seat at the library with *The Shining*. When I finished chapter six, I grabbed my journal and bolted to the librarian's desk.

"Mom, what's a caul birth?"

"Why are you asking about that now?" she askied, and I showed her the reference to caul births and second sight in chapter six.

"I'd forgotten that part," she said. "A caul birth is when a baby is born with the amniotic sac over its head. It kind of looks like a pillowcase. You were a caul birth, you know? That's why I call you my lucky one."

"Pillowhead!" I exclaimed, looking right at her.

"That's right. Pillowhead. In a way, it's your brothers' sideways compliment."

I rolled my eyes.

"Can you help me find more information about caul babies?"

"A caul birth is rare, and a sign of good luck," she said as she handed me a piece of paper listing a number of titles and their Dewey Decimal numbers. I spent the next two hours taking detailed notes in my journal from several books she helped me pull off the shelves, most of them from the occult and superstition section of the library.

After I finished the last one, I turned to a clean page in my journal. I couldn't write fast enough, my hand barely keeping up with my thoughts. The scribbles became bigger and messier than my normal handwriting. I had so many questions to add to the back of my journal.

Danny in *The Shining* was a caul baby, and he saw ghosts. He knew things he wasn't supposed to know. I know things. I feel things. Things I probably shouldn't know.
Do I shine like Danny?
Is my unzipping a shining?

Dave and Andrew call me Pillowhead. They tease me about the "pillowcase" and "hood" I never really took off. They say that I live my life still under the veil that had to be cut off my head at birth.

The Shadow's Shine

Do babies born with a caul really have "second sight"?
Do I have a second sight?
Is the Shadow a ghost?
If so, who was he in life?

CHAPTER ELEVEN

Sunglasses At Night

That night, I fell asleep under the covers with my flashlight and my library copy of *The Shining*. I had the nightmare again, with one significant difference. When I closed the medicine cabinet, this time, I saw myself in the mirror with a slimy hood over my face, my own caul. I could see clearly, but as I peeled the caul away from my face, the mirror got foggy. Then, the Shadow reached over my shoulder and wrote the word REDRUM in the fogged-up mirror. When the decaying old woman climbed out of the bathtub, she had a caul over her eyes and nose, but not her sewn-shut mouth. I reached over my head to pull my own caul back over my face.

I awoke in a sweaty terror, and filled three more pages of my journal with "it's just a dream."

But, I didn't feel any better.

There was no way I was going back to sleep that night, so I got up and got dressed. I took my flashlight and went outside. It was about 4:00 a.m. The crickets chirping comforted me. The wind in the trees soothed me.

An owl called to me from the backyard woods.

I didn't really know where I was going. I just walked. Lightning bugs, like fairies in the forest, showed me the way as I chased them with the ray of my flashlight.

I found the owl perched on Excalibur. I caught its yellow eyes in the shine of my flashlight, and it quickly flew away. Then I realized where I was. Where I wasn't supposed to be, at the base of the Joint. I hadn't seen it since my brothers started working on it two weeks earlier. It was almost done.

The tree fort now had two entrances, as the original trap door was still there. Dave and Andrew had added a real ladder, with rails and rungs that led up to a front porch with a real door. There were walls, a full roof, and even a couple windows. The trap door was open, and light poured down like a spotlight onto a new rope ladder winding down the trunk of the tree. I heard soft whistling.

Who was in there?

Dave and Andrew? Working in the middle of the night?

That couldn't've been just the wind.

The whistling called to me in the same way the owl did. I felt like an entranced cartoon character, with spiraled eyes. I no longer had control of my thoughts or actions. I just followed the whistled song as it pulled me up the ladder like a marionette on strings.

I'm not supposed to be up here.

Who is in there?

Three flashlights were strung from the ceiling to point down at the center of the tree fort. It took me a couple seconds before I realized it was Teddy sitting under the glow of the lights. I hadn't seen him in two weeks. He looked ghostly. He looked like he hadn't changed clothes, showered, slept, or eaten that entire time.

If there were any such thing as undead, or mostly dead, or nearly dead, that's what I was looking at. He looked like he had just come out of a scene from the end of *Ghostbusters*. He wore a ratty t-shirt and very dirty jeans. His black eye had almost completely healed, but he had a fresh fat lip and a gash on his chin. He was still wearing the wrist brace.

Had Teddy not slept at all since Murphy died?

Did he poke the bear again?

Did the bear fight back?

But that wasn't the scary part.

The scary part was what he was doing.

He was skinning a rabbit.

The stench was so overwhelming I could barely breathe, and my throat tightened. I wanted to ask if he was okay, but I couldn't get myself to move a muscle, much less speak.

He looked up, right at me, and I gasped.

I take that back; he wasn't looking at me. His gaze was empty, like his thoughts were far away. It was as if he was looking up from his work, deep in thought, and looked right through me instead of at me.

Silence.

We stared at each other for more than 10 seconds, which doesn't sound like a long time, only a fraction of a minute, but in that moment, it felt like an eternity. Then, he seemed to wake up and offered me a tiny head nod of acknowledgement. Then he flipped the sunglasses perched on top of his head onto his face and started whistling the tune to *Sunglasses at Night*.

I was stunned. I couldn't move. I just stayed there, watching him for I don't know how much longer.

He had nailed the rabbit by the ears and legs onto a wood block and sliced down its belly. A gaping hole in the gut revealed what the bucket next to him most likely contained. Soft grey tufts of fur were everywhere, stuck in Teddy's hair, clinging to puddles of blood on the floor, drifting through the window.

He looked rather serene. He peeled the skin away from the rabbit's ribs, using the pocketknife to slice the connecting tissue. He looked like an expert, skilled with the knife and his grip on the pelt as he peeled. The precision and the care he took reminded me of how he dissected the mouse in the bathtub. Despite the ugliness of the scene, he looked curious, intent, absorbed in his task.

He wasn't disturbed in the least bit that I had caught him. He didn't even seem to care that I watched. Rather, he looked like Kevin or Tommy did when one of us walked in on them playing video games, gaze glued to the screen. He had to know I was there, he had nodded at me, but after he looked back down, he didn't look up at me again. He was too consumed.

Then it happened.

The unzipping.

My shining turned on.

It startled me at first, the rush of cold tingles through the gap in my back, forcing a slow, deep nostril gasp of air into my lungs like a vacuum. Now that I knew what it was, I wasn't as scared by it. I surrendered to it. My Shining.

In that moment, I was overwhelmed with the feeling of, well, *curiosity,* like glitter dumping out of a bottle all over the floor. The scene in front of me was not ugly or gory anymore, but rather intriguing. Then I got a flash vision in my mind, of a much older Teddy standing in a sterile hospital room wearing a lab coat, in med school, preparing for a cadaver lab. Suddenly, I was the one staring off into space, to a distance far away.

As suddenly as it opened, my back zipped back up, the curiosity evaporated, and the medical lab vision blew away like a tuft of rabbit fur out the window. Quietly, I tiptoed my way back down the rope ladder. When I got to the bottom, I sat on the ground, leaned up against the tree and listened to the crickets and the wind, and Teddy's whistling, wishing I had a pair of sunglasses of my own to wear.

Would sunglasses at night be like wearing a caul?

Opening up the second sight?

And then the whistling stopped.

Teddy poked his head down through the trap door through the floor of the treehouse, hanging himself upside down from inside the little tree fort. The sunglasses fell off his head and landed on the ground next to me.

Ask and I shall receive.

I picked up the sunglasses and put them on my face. The world looked different, wearing sunglasses at night. It looked, well, somehow sharper. While darker, it was also oddly clearer.

"Hey, Alex," Teddy said in his happy-go-lucky voice.

"Huh?" I could barely push the burp of a word out of my throat.

"Happy Birthday!" He looked right at me. His head was upside down, and his too-long hair was standing on end, upside down.

Then, he started whistling again as he pulled his head back up and shut the trap door.

My unzipping opened back up.

Um, yeah . . . Happy birthday to me?

I sat there at the base of the tree, my unzipped back pressed up against the trunk. Sunglasses on my face. I stayed there, not really thinking about anything. I didn't really feel anything either. If anything, I went into this quiet, still space, of, well, nothingness. Like those times at school where I'd zone out and didn't hear the teacher or the other kids in class, I'd just sort of stare out the window and go somewhere else for a while. I just can't tell you where somewhere else is, unless it is some kind of nowhere-ville. While my body sat at the base of the tree, my mind went blank for I don't know how long. It actually felt kind of nice.

"Hey." Teddy woke me from my cozy trance when he came down from the tree fort some time later, as the sun started rising.

"Hey." I didn't know what to say as he sat down next to me. He leaned up against the tree with his legs out long and crossed. He looked comfortable, nonchalant.

"You're still here." He pulled bloody surgical gloves off his hands and shoved them in his pocket.

"I'm still here."

"You like the shades, huh?" He pushed them up my nose for me.

"Yeah. They're nice." I took them off my face and held them out to him. I didn't really want to return them. Their extra layer of darkness was really comforting.

"Keep 'em."

Grateful, I put them back on my face.

Silence.

And then my mind went CRAZY, the opposite of the nothingness I had just enjoyed. Thoughts and questions ping-ponged and monkey-hopped all over the inside of my skull. I could almost feel them bounce like super balls between my ears.

What were you doing up there? Were you actually skinning a rabbit? And WHY? What happened to your lip? Your chin? Your eye? Your wrist? Did someone beat you up? What did the bear do? Are you okay? Why are you so skinny? How did I not notice you were this skinny before? Do you have insomnia? Does your mom know you are out here? Does Tommy know you are doing this? How many times have you been up there? How long have you been coming out here in the middle of the night? Who ARE you? Do I even know you? Is this all 'cause of Murphy? Or have you always been like this? How many other animals have you dissected? How come you haven't talked to me about this?

"Are we gonna talk about it?" I finally said out loud.

"Do you want to?" he asked.

"Do you want to?" I asked back.

"I'm not sure."

"Me neither."

We sat in silence for a while as the questions continued to bump around in my head.

"I have so many questions," I finally said.

"I probably don't have any answers for you."

"I don't know if I really want to know the answers."

Silence.

"Can I ask just one?"

"Sure."

"Are you okay?" I asked, emphasizing the word *okay*.

"Yeah. At least, I think I am."

"You don't look okay."

"Well thanks for that." He elbowed me in the ribs.

"I mean it, Teddy. You look like hell."

"I know." He looked down, and took a long breath before he continued.

"I'm not sleeping. I mean, not at all. I have these spans of time where I kinda lose time. I come up here without thinking about it, and I do things without really *deciding* to do anything. It's more like I'm just watching myself do things. I don't think. I don't feel. It's just sort of empty. Then I come back to myself, like now."

"I'm worried about you."

"I know. But really, I feel fine."

He smiled at me. He looked like my best friend again, but different.

A hundred more questions bubbled inside my throat like the effervescent foam of the first sip of a freshly opened can of pop. I couldn't' swallow the thoughts, but I couldn't let them out my mouth either. The questions just buzzed around in my mouth and throat. Some even climbed up my nose, making my eyes water. He probably had just as many questions himself. I was just happy to have my friend with me in that moment.

"Can I ask one more question?"

"I'd rather you didn't."

"Okay."

I took a long breath, blowing out my exhale like I was smoking, hoping the questions might escape on my breath. They didn't, but they did slow down a little.

"I've missed you, Teddy."

I laid my head on his shoulder.

"I know. I miss me too."

He laid his head on top of mine.

Something in me told me to remember that moment forever.

"You all right?" he asked, pointing to my knee. I hadn't even realized I had scraped it while climbing up the ladder.

"Yeah, just a little scrape," I said, picking the dirt out of the wound.

"That doesn't look so good."

"It's fine, really," I said, leaning forward to blow on the scrape.

"Are you sure?"

"It's fine," I said again, pulling my hair out of my ponytail to re-tie it back. A wisp of hair fell into my wound and stuck as I was trying to tie my hair and blow on the wound at the same time.

"Careful," Teddy said, pulling the wisps of hair away from the wound. Then, his hand rested on the side of my face, and the next thing I knew, he looked me right in the eye.

Then it happened.

It happened quicker than I realized what was even happening. His lips were there, little pillows just barely touching mine, but leaving an electric tingling in their wake.

Thoughts pelleted my brain like machine gun fire, so fast that I couldn't really enjoy or even pay attention to what was happening.

Teddy kissed me!

My first kiss ever.

TEDDY!

This was my friend, my buddy, kissing ME!

This kid I had known for most of my life.

A kid I would sit next to in school this fall.

He kissed me.

...

And I liked it.

I leaned toward him. And it happened again.

This time, his lips lingered. They didn't just touch my lips, they melted into mine. It took my breath away. I didn't know the first thing about kissing and breathing. As I stopped breathing, so did time.

Should I hold my breath?

Should I close my eyes?

If I leave my eyes open, where do I look?

Just about the time I realized my eyes had been closed the whole time, his lips trailed away. But I wanted more. My lips parted slightly, puffing up, reaching out for his. And then, a third time, his lips on mine. But this time, they were wet.

I didn't know kisses were wet.

Wait, is that?

Oh my God, that's his tongue!

Then everything turned to mist.

All I could feel were the pillows of our lips and the zinging tingle of his tongue.

We made out for a really long time.

And not long enough.

When it was over, Teddy leaned his head back against the tree. Breathless, I realized I had held my breath for most of the time. I didn't want to gasp, so I took long, slow, silent sips of air, trying to calm the heavy pattering. I realized my hand was on his thigh, and his was on my knee.

CHAPTER TWELVE

Birthday

I sneaked back into the house and fixed myself a bowl of oatmeal. I hadn't had two bites before Dave came in the back door with Andrew close on his heels.

"Drat, she's already up!" Dave said.

"Happy Birthday, Pillowhead," Andrew said.

"You ruined our surprise," Dave said.

"What surprise?" I asked.

"We were gonna make a true pillowhead out of you and carry you out to see your birthday present," Andrew said, while tossing the pillowcase in his hands over his shoulder.

"Your grand birthday plan was to abduct me like a scene in a horror film?"

"Yup." Andrew tossed the pillowcase on the kitchen table. I shoved a spoonful of oatmeal into my mouth, hoping it would muffle the secret that I'd already been out to see it.

"They're lying to you," Dad said as he came into the kitchen with Mom close behind him. "The tree fort isn't quite ready yet."

"You were out there?" Andrew asked.

"Yup," Dad said. "It's looking good."

"That porch looks rather dangerous, boys. It needs a railing," Mom said.

"It'll be done by dinner time tonight," Dave said.

I shoved another spoonful of oatmeal in my mouth.

"We are gonna string up a rope railing, kinda like macramé," Andrew added.

"Oh, that would be cool," Dad said.

"You and your friends aren't allowed up there until they finish the railing, is that understood?" Dad said in his stern, fatherly voice.

I nodded.

"And you boys must finish the railing before we do cake and candles tonight."

"That's the plan, Dad."

Just as I chewed and swallowed the last bite of oatmeal with my secret, I was saved by a knock at the back door.

It was Tommy, swinging his slingshot around the full circumference of his arm.

"Hey Alex, happy birthday!"

"Thanks," I said, placing my oatmeal bowl in the sink.

"You two are not allowed to go to the tree fort yet," Dad instructed.

"I know," I said, walking out with Tommy and pulling the door shut behind me.

"Is Teddy gonna come out today?" I asked, hoping our middle of the night rendezvous might have changed things for Teddy.

"Prolly not," Tommy said, his voice turning down. He missed Teddy as much as I did.

"Where's Kevin?"

"They went to the cabin for a couple weeks."

"Stink House?" I suggested.

He nodded.

The whole walk there he gave me a blow-by-blow description of beating the next level of Super Mario Bros. I listened without really paying attention. Still talking, Tommy climbed up first. From the top, he reached his hand down to me to help me up the last step.

"I got it," I said, refusing his hand.

The whole scene was rather awkward. The last step up the Stink House was the biggest one. Teddy, Tommy, and Kevin were all taller than me and could sort of push themselves up like climbing out of a swimming pool. But I was shorter. I needed to grab the lip of the roof with both hands and do a half pull-up in order to swing my other leg up to the roof, which was almost at my shoulder height. I had a system. It worked for me. Tommy's assistance didn't fit in my system.

"Let me help you."

"No, I got it," I said more firmly.

"I want to help you."

And that's where it got really awkward. I refused his hand and swung my leg over the side. He reached to grab my shoulder and ended up with a fistful of my shirt. The way he was positioned meant his feet were in my way. Needing to roll my center of gravity, my bottom foot hovered just above the brick and my upper leg gripped to the roof, but I was stuck in this awkward hovering place.

"You gotta move," I insisted.

"I've got you."

He pulled at my shirt, which only served to reposition my shirt, not my body.

"You gotta move so I can get up," I said again.

Instead of moving, he sat down and grabbed at my shoulder with both his hands. As he tugged, he leaned back, finally giving me enough to space to shift my weight so I was firmly on the roof and could lift my bottom leg up. But, it meant I rolled almost on top of him.

And then, he kissed me.

My lips stayed flat, still . . . stiff, even.

Not at all like they were with Teddy.

Not even close.

Too stunned to react, I didn't kiss him back, but I didn't pull away either. I just froze. My heart pounded as if it were on the outside of my shirt.

"I'm sorry," he said as he leaned away, putting his hands up like a robber caught by a cop.

"It's okay," I said.

I didn't want to make Tommy feel bad, but I also didn't want to stick around either. Without even thinking about it, I just turned around and scurried back down the Stink House wall.

"Seriously, I'm sorry."

"It's okay. Just weird."

"Do you want me to leave you alone?"

"No. It's fine, Tommy, really. Just drop it."

"Okay."

We walked in silence back to the houses, but he kept a good distance behind me, occasionally loading stones into his slingshot and stopping to shoot them. Finally, as we meandered along the dried-up creek bed, I broke the silence.

"Tommy, is Teddy okay?"

"I don't know," he said, crouching down to find another stone.

"I'm worried about him."

"He's been doing some really weird things since Murphy died," Tommy said, loading another stone into his slingshot. "I mean, *weird* stuff."

Did Tommy know what I knew?

"Like what?"

"He's been sneaking out of the house every night," he said, shooting another stone. This one didn't hit anything.

"To do what?" I gathered a few stones and handed them to Tommy. I needed something to distract myself, to occupy my hands. I didn't want Tommy to see me react.

"I don't know. I don't think he's sleeping. I mean . . . he's not sleeping . . . AT ALL."

He took a moment to load another stone into his slingshot before continuing his thought.

"Mom says that he just needs time."

"What do you think he does when he sneaks out every night?" I asked, crouching down to dig a couple more stones out of the dirt.

"I don't know. I try not to think about it."

Tommy squinted one eye shut as he aimed another stone towards a tree limb. Then both eyes squinted, like he was trying to squint away the truth.

I kept walking along the trail, my head down, while Tommy crouched down a few steps behind me to find another stone.

I heard the slingshot pull back farther than before.

CRACK!

Even though I knew what it was, the sound made me jump. It was louder than the others, and I felt it deeper inside me. I instinctively looked back over my left shoulder at Tommy behind me. Then, before I knew what was happening, words spewed out of my mouth like a geyser, erupting before they even thoughts formed in my head.

"When Angry Man killed Murphy, Teddy died too."

Why did I just say that?

I covered my mouth with both my hands, trying to shove the words back in.

I tripped and landed on my knees. I looked back at Tommy, worried about how he might react. At first I thought the look was rage, that he was mad at me. The look behind his eyes was something I had never seen before. But then, I realized he wasn't looking at me at all. Rather, he looked *through* me, at something in the distance. I didn't see what he saw. But I saw his face, and it was fear. No, it was more than fear. It was terror.

I froze. Tommy's terror spilled all over me. My limbs were sucked into the ground, like roots growing into the soil. At the same time, all my strength and coordination flew away like a flock of birds. Everything sped up and slowed down all at the same time. Fast forward and slow motion.

CHAPTER THIRTEEN

An Army of Ghosts

Tommy took off running. In fast forward. And he screamed, like the screech of an eagle. Terror. It was the most ear piercing noise I had ever heard. come out of a human being. And it didn't stop, the screech just went on and on and on. I felt the sound scratch along the inside of my bones, like fingernails down a chalkboard. The fray of my nervous system paralyzed me. I pushed my fingers so deep into my ears that I could almost taste my bitter earwax on the back of my tongue. Then, Tommy disappeared in a fog, running in slow motion, his shrieks muffled into silence.

Amidst the foggy whiteness, the Shadow emerged.

He stood just a few feet from me and nodded at me.

I nodded back.

"*I have something important to show you.*"

The Shadow grabbed my wrist and yanked on my arm so hard that it felt like he might pull it right out of the socket. I felt like a toddler in trouble. He moved faster than my stumbling legs could keep up.

Then, he stopped.

Slow Motion.

He let go of my wrist, and dragged his long, pointy fingernail tip down the back of my head, melting through my scalp like soft wax. My shining unzipped, and once again, I fell to my hands and knees.

Then, he pointed up.

Sunlight.

Is that . . .?

Squint.

No, it can't be.

Branches.

That's not for real.

Blink.

It is . . .

That's when I saw what Tommy saw.

I couldn't unsee it.

Teddy.

Impaled on Excalibur.

Face down.

Several feet up from the ground.

Pierced through his midsection.

His head, legs, and arms dangling.

Completely limp.

Lifeless.

His eyes were open, a blank, empty stare. His mouth was open. He wasn't wearing a shirt, and there wasn't much blood.

I tried to scream but nothing more than a faint squeak came out of my mouth. With that squeak, the last bit of my strength and coordination fluttered out of my mouth like a butterfly. I collapsed into fetal position amongst the tree roots and leaves and breathed in the dank odor of earth. My hands clasped tightly over my eyes trying to block out Teddy's stare. Like the icy stare of Medusa, Teddy's empty stare froze me into stone.

Death smelled like earth, the dank scent of decaying wet-soil leaves. I cried, but not normal tears, the tears wouldn't squeeze out. Rather, they burned lava tubes down the inside my skull, from the corners of my eyes down my sinuses to the back of my nose and throat. A sting I wish I could forget. But like Tommy's eagle scream, earth's death smell, and Teddy's Medusa stare, I couldn't un-smell, un-hear, or un-see what I just felt.

The sting was too much. I had to let them out. I couldn't *not* look. I opened my eyes and squinted through the tiny hazy gap between my fingers. A portal window into another realm, a parallel universe. Everything was foggy, like cataracts, a white haze through the salt-watery film of tears that refused to spill out of my eyes. I saw things that were there, but not there. Real, but not real, in colors and textures that don't exist in the Earthly realm. Eventually, I dropped my hands from my face, and let the foggy haze consume me, surrendering to the not-real reality.

The other shadow, the one with the shackles, flew like a giant vulture around Teddy's limp body, making huge swooping circles around Excalibur, sometimes grazing his tattered cloak on the ground, and sometimes spiraling high up into the sky. Sometimes he swerved and swooped rapidly, and other times he moved in slow motion, or even hovered.

More shadows, a massive army of ghosts loomed over us. While they looked scary with their wrinkled faces, ragged cloaks, and heavy hoods, when I really looked at them, and how they were moving or not moving, there was kindness there—a kindness and softness like I had never known before. Their cloaks were all different colors. Beautiful colors. Amazing Technicolor Dream Coat colors.

Some of the ghosts stood around the base of Excalibur, wearing heavy armor under their cloaks, holding long staffs. Others hovered in the background, leaning against trees, arms crossed, men in waiting. Still others perched in the trees like fairies, brightly colored bursts of glittery light, holding space. Others circled in the sky around Teddy, like a flock of birds playing in the current.

The Shadow draped himself and his heavy, scratchy, wool cloak over me. The volume of the world turned down to zero until eventually, what muffled sounds hadn't been drowned out by the fog were completely silenced with the weight of his wool cloak. Then he curled up behind me, cupping my head in his hand. His scratchy, breathy voice navigated its way down the windy tubes of my ear canals to tap-tap-tap on my eardrums with a bubble pop tickle.

"I'm here now, and I'll never leave you alone, ever again."

I opened my hand and invited his gnarly, wrinkled fingers to lace with mine.

It felt like Teddy's hand.

CHAPTER FOURTEEN

Silence

"Alex!?" Dave's far away muffled voice smeared the unreal world away like a dirty chalkboard eraser leaving a dusty trail of white streaks.

Tommy tugged and pulled at my shirt as he gagged and spit like he wanted to vomit but couldn't. I tried to get up, but my feet slipped underneath me. My weight pulled Tommy to the ground with me.

Dave scooped me up in his arms and carried me home. Tommy stumbled over his own feet next to him. I kept saying Teddy's name, but I'm not sure if I was screaming or whispering, or if any sound came out at all.

When we got to our back porch, Mom came out from the kitchen as Dave put me down and disappeared into the kitchen. Tommy collapsed at my feet.

"Are you okay?" Mom asked.

I shook my head. Tommy struggled to catch his breath.

"What happened?" she asked while trying to tend to my scraped knees, but I pushed her hands away. Neither of us had words. With our tongues tied, we weren't able to answer her. Tommy managed to breathe out one word with each gasp.

"Teddy . . . fell . . . Excalibur."

He had barely finished his last unintelligible word when Dave appeared again, the kitchen phone cord stretched to its limit winding from the kitchen through the mud room and out the back door of the house.

Tommy stood up and started to stumble back toward the Joint, but Dave grabbed him, handing the phone to Mom.

"You can't go back there," Dave said.

"Teddy!" Tommy sobbed.

"That's not a good idea."

Tommy kicked both his legs as hard as he could to get away from Dave, but Dave held him so tightly in a big bear hug around his middle that Tommy's legs just flailed in the air.

"What happened?" Andrew asked, walking around the side of the house from the garage.

"Go make sure Mrs. James stays away from the Joint." Dave said firmly, still holding Tommy.

"What happened?" Andrew asked again.

"Teddy fell," he gave Andrew a look that said enough for Andrew to know the seriousness of the situation. Andrew ran like a cartoon character leaving behind a swirl of dirt while Mom paced back and forth from the kitchen to the porch, tugging at the phone cord.

"Someone's gotta go be with Teddy!" Tommy screamed, clawing at Dave's face, feet kicking off the ground. Dave talked to

Tommy in a deep, slow drawl like you see on movies, but Tommy's arms and legs continued to flail at high speed.

I sat cross-legged on the floor of our back deck, wanting it all to stop.

Mom was on the phone.

Dave was holding Tommy.

Andrew had disappeared into the James's house.

I was free.

I ran.

I ran at a full sprint.

My legs moved faster than I knew they could take me.

All I wanted to do was get to Teddy.

To be with him.

To hold his hand.

To tell him everything was gonna be all right.

But everything wasn't all right.

The sky was falling.

Everything would change now. Everyone and everything and the entire world switched on me, like a dream that isn't real but feels real, and you know it's not real, and then you realize it isn't a dream, but it is, because it wouldn't feel and sound and look so strange if it weren't.

But this was real.

All of it.

So real, it was unreal.

There he was, still hanging in mid-air, suspended on the blade of Excalibur. Once again, on my knees, I looked up at Teddy. And then I closed my eyes, and everything stopped. The whirring sound was gone. The sky stopped spinning. The trees stopped moving. My head stopped hurting.

Everything just stopped.

And everything was beautiful.

Hauntingly beautiful.

And terrifying.

There's always some kind of sound, a quiet sound of life being lived. The white noise of the furnace in big buildings, or the quiet rustle of leaves in the wind, or even the sniffling and coughing of the person sitting next to me during a test at school.

But at that moment, that very brief moment when I was alone in the woods, eye closed, kneeling below Teddy, I heard what complete silence feels like. I couldn't even hear myself breathe.

Was I breathing?

Did I die too?

Behind my closed eyelids I saw Teddy's blank, dead face.

There is nothing in the world more terrifying than complete silence.

In silence, everything is too true.

I opened my eyes, and everything spun again.

With my eyes open, I could hear the world spinning on its axis. It was spinning too fast and the whirring was so loud it covered up all other sounds. At the same time, the sky seemed to be spinning on its own axis separate from that of the Earth. Each tree was spinning in its own direction as well. The whirring became a whine, like a really loud refrigerator. The sound was working from the inside out, almost like my ears were making the noise and hearing it at the same time.

I closed my eyes. The spinning stopped. Silence.

But, Teddy's dead stare. Still. Silent. Vacant.

I opened my eyes, plugged my ears, and hummed to myself.

That only made the world spin faster, the noises louder.

I closed my eyes.

Teddy. The horror.

The quiet was less painful than the spinning, so I kept my eyes closed.

The leaves of the old oak branches bent toward the leaves and branches of the other trees refusing to touch. Canopy shyness. They left just enough space for rays of sunlight to peek between them and shine on Teddy. In that, I found comfort, so I let my imagination take over

"Hey Alex?" he looked down at me while swimming his limbs through the deep end of the clear blue sky. "Could you help me off of this thing? It's not exactly comfortable." He laughed.

"You're such a klutz," I joked back.

"I am NOT a klutz." He stopped swimming and glared at me instead, dead serious.

"It's Angry Man. I'm not a klutz. It's always been Angry Man."

I saw a flash of Teddy's injuries.

Crutches for a broken ankle last summer.

Stitches in his chin at Christmas.

The wrist brace when school started last fall.

Murphy's lifeless body in the middle of the street.

His black eye and wrist brace.

The fat lip he had while skinning the rabbit.

And then—I knew.

"Angry Man is your—"

"Don't say it out loud!" he snapped.

I shut my mouth and swallowed.

Angry Man.

Teddy poked the bear.

And the bear got mad.

Too mad.

And then, my tiny moment of aloneness ended.

"MY BABY!" Mrs. James screamed, running toward me with Andrew chasing behind her.

As Mrs. James came toward me, half running and half crawling, tripping over every other step, I caught a glimpse of what she had probably looked like as a little girl. I don't know if it was her state or the look in her eyes, but I almost thought she was five years old, crying after taking a tumble off her two-wheeler for the first time. She didn't have any shoes on, and her knees and hands were as cut up and bloody as my own. When she collapsed next to me on the ground, her wails silenced.

Andrew positioned himself between us and Teddy's body, intending, I suppose, to obscure our view. He put his left hand on his hip in almost an authoritative-strict-teacher sort of way, while his right hand stroked his forehead between his forefinger and thumb, pulling and pinching at the skin.

I crawled over to her, and she pulled me to her. She expanded in size from the five-year-old back to the full-size mother, only bigger. She straddled her legs around me from behind and wrapped her arms around my shoulders. She rested her head on mine, her wispy red hair tickling my neck. I hugged my knees to my chest and buried my face in her arm. I felt her tears drip down my arm.

Once again, the world fell silent, and time evaporated.

When Tommy appeared next to us, Mrs. James pulled Tommy into the womb of her body with me. Her hands on our heads, she buried her face in our hair. The three of us rocked together as one unit, shuddering in silent sobs.

Off in the distance, the wail of approaching sirens cried for us.

CHAPTER FIFTEEN

The Great Horned Owl

That night when I climbed into bed, I didn't sleep.

I had too many questions and nowhere to put them.

The questions squiggled around in my head. Like worm squiggles leaving fossil imprints on the inside of my skull, the questions looked for answers to attach to their backs as wings so they could fly away, back to wherever they came from. They multiplied exponentially, building pressure in my head.

There were too many of them, and no way to pop them. I even tried plugging my nose, squeezing my eyes shut and blowing, in hopes of pushing them out my ears with my breath. But nothing happened. So, I opened my mouth and tried to scream, or wail, or moan . . . but nothing came out.

The question marks multiplied.

The pressure built.

I needed to cry.

For the first time, I actually wanted my unzipping to happen. Maybe, just maybe, if my neck and spine unzipped, the salty waters could spill out and have someplace to go. I needed some kind of release, relief.

Curled in a fetal position, gripping my head in my hands, I wished for that heebie-jeebie tingle of discomfort to zing down my spine and open the gate. But, my unzipping didn't happen.

And then . . .

CRACK!

Thunder.

A blinding flash of lightning, followed almost immediately by a deafening clap of thunder that jolted me right off the bed. I landed on the floor with a *thud*. As much as I hoped the rumbles would shake the question pressures out of me, they didn't. They just wriggled and squiggled more, matching the low, distant thunder. By this time, the thoughts in my head were no longer complete sentences, just phrases and single words, all with question marks attached. The house shuddered, trembling from another loud rumble.. Oddly, I found the vibrations of the floorboards underneath me comforting. When the rumbling stopped, I got up off the floor and looked out the window.

Whoooo. Whooooo. Who.

My owl, the same one who had led me to Teddy and his sunglasses at night, called to me.

Where was she?

That one question somehow took power over all the other questions in my head. It had a different energy, perhaps because it was something I could follow to an answer. I put on my fuzzy slippers and my oversized terrycloth robe and tiptoed down the stairs, avoiding the creaky floorboards through the kitchen to our back deck.

Whoooo. Whooooo. Who.

She was close. Very close.

As if on cue, just as I stepped off the bottom step of our back deck, at precisely the end of her last call, another flash of lightning revealed the owl perched on top of my rickety-old unused swing set. Her great horns, illuminated by the lightning, looked almost like a crown. Thunder rumbled softly in the distance like it was beckoning me to follow.

Whoooo. Who. Whooooooo.

Her call comforted me even more than the thunder. Each hoot slowed the churning of the worm questions in my skull.

I walked out toward her.

I sat down and started to swing, dragging my slippered toes on the dirt ground, gazing up at her just a few feet above my head.

Who. Whooo. Whoooo.

She looked down at me.

I looked up at her.

"Why?" I whispered, half expecting her to fly away.

She stayed.

I wondered if I had actually spoken, or if my voice remained stuck behind my tongue, hidden somewhere with my cries and screams. Whether I had actually spoken out loud or not didn't matter, somehow I felt that she had heard me.

Who. Who. Who. Whoooo.

Where's Teddy now?

Whooo. Whooo.

Am I gonna be okay?

Who. Who. Who. Whooo. Who.

What's gonna happen now?

Whooooo. Whooooooooo. Who. Whoooooo.

Her responses were so simple. The language of nature. Her soothing, soft staccato of sounds didn't end in question marks. Rather, each call ended in periods, an ellipsis, trailing off into a quiet distance. The question marks in my brain stilled, elongating into their own ellipses. Her hoots softened everything inside me into a smooth trickle, very similar to the soft, spitting spurts of trickling rain spilling from the sky.

If I stopped chasing the questions and trying to catch their answers, but rather just let them do what they wanted to do, they would find their own way to settle. My owl showed me in her repetitive *who* that questions just lead to more questions. And that was okay.

I didn't need to know the answers to my questions.

There weren't answers anyway.

It's okay to have more questions.

The answers aren't the point.

And somehow, the pressure was gone.

I didn't feel the need to cry anymore.

Thank you.

Who. Who. Who.

CRACK!

As if on cue, punctuating the end of my conversation with the great horned owl, lightning flashed and thunder cracked simultaneously.

My owl silently flew away.

And the sky opened up.

The sky cried for me.

Big, slobbery, wet sheets of grief-ridden rain poured out of the sky. My terrycloth robe tripled in weight. My hair clung in long streaks to my face and neck. My fuzzy slippers became sloshing blotches dragging through the mud beneath the swing.

I stood up from the swing, opened my arms wide to the sky, and opened my mouth.

Finally, sound came out.

It was the first sound to escape my lips since the moment Tommy saw Teddy on Excalibur. At first, the sound was a loud, wailing scream, similar to the screech of Tommy's eagle screams. But mine was more eerie and raspy, more like a barn owl. Like the sound I would expect from the Shadow as he flies. Then, the noise from my throat took shape and form. The same words, the raw, razor-edged truth that I had shoved back down my throat after spitting them at Tommy, erupted and tumbled off my tongue in a burning lava spill.

"WHEN ANGRY MAN KILLED MURPHY, TEDDY DIED TOO!"

And then I collapsed to the ground.

Splayed open on the ground.

I sobbed. Loud guttural wails waterfalled out of my mouth like the rain spilling from the sky. My whole body cried until I couldn't tell what was rain and what was tears. I didn't know the difference between my shuddering sobs and thunder rumbles.

The rain came down in heavy sheets. The grass beneath me was saturated, a giant, green carpet puddle. It was warm rain with an occasional whoosh of wind. Blinking away the rain and my tears was impossible, so I finally just let my eyes close as tears squeezed out of their corners and dribbled down to my ears. I couldn't tell if I was still crying anyway; my tears blended with the rain, and my voice got lost in the whipping of the wind.

As quickly as the rain started, it stopped, and I went back inside the house.

In the bathroom, I peeled off my soaked robe and pajamas, balled them up, and shoved them down the laundry chute until I heard them *splat* on the concrete floor of the basement laundry room. I wrapped myself up in three towels: One on my head, one around my waist, and an over-sized beach towel wrapped twice around my shoulders like a blanket. I tiptoed back up the stairs around the creaky floorboards, and back to my bedroom.

I changed into a fresh pair of pajamas, sat down at my desk, and took out an old sketchpad and a pack of colored pencils.

I started with the questions in the back of my journal. They took the shape of the giant oak tree that held the Joint. The words changed colors from the brown and grey trunk to the tan branches and green leaves. Sometimes, each leaf was just one word, a whole question in itself. Sometimes, a question took up a whole branch. Questions with more words made up the dozens of leaves spilling out of the tree. Some questions floated in the sky in various shades of blue and pink, while others twinkled on the ground like dew and grass. At times they gushed out of me, in sloppy letters forming shaky and quivering lines inside the image of the tree. Other times they trickled, in slow methodical phrasings, precisely placed.

Several hours later, I ripped the page from the spiral bound notebook and carefully pulled off the hanging tabs from the edge, one by one. Just as I plucked off the last tab, I heard Mom and Dad in the kitchen.

The next thing I knew, I was in the kitchen too.

Andrew stood at the stove, stirring a pot of oatmeal, and Dave leaned against the refrigerator drinking a cup of coffee. Mom and Dad sat at the table sipping coffee.

The Shadow in his dense wool cloak, lurked in the corner by the stove.

What was usually a busy bustling kitchen full of voices and noises was eerily quiet.

I placed my question tree in front of Mom at the table and sat down at the seat farthest from her. Dave caught my eye and put his coffee cup on top of the fridge, squeezed his way behind our brother at the stove, and wrapped me up in a hug. Andrew spooned oatmeal from the stove into my favorite cereal bowl and placed it in front of me.

Mom traced her fingers gently along the branches and leaves as she read. Dad sat next to her, his hand on her knee, reading over her shoulder. Big, wet tears bubbled out of their eyes and snaked down their cheeks. As they read, and I ate, I watched the expressions on their faces reveal even more questions, like cartoon balloon bubbles popping over their heads. I didn't know what their questions were, but I could tell that they had ones that I didn't have.

"It's really beautiful," Mom finally said, long after Dad and Dave and Andrew had left the kitchen.

"Thanks, I think?" I said.

"It really is one of the most beautiful pieces of artwork I've ever seen."

She put her cup down and looked me right in the eye, reaching across the table for my hand.

"Thanks," I said, letting her hand rest on top of mine.

"It's the most honest expressions of grief I have ever seen in my entire life."

My eyes filled up wet. Suddenly I felt raw, exposed, more vulnerable than I knew how to be. Salty wetness spilled down the front of my cheeks without the rain to dilute it, then the wetness turned to hot, red fire, ripping through the inside back of my throat, scratching at my heart, and burning down my face.

I unzipped. But it wasn't just an unzipping this time. The zippered teeth ripped apart at the seams, the shrieking of metal being pulled away from metal running all the way down my spine.

"I CAN'T TALK ABOUT IT NOW!" I slammed my bowl on the table, grabbed the question tree off the table, crumpled it into a ball, and threw it at Mom before running out the back door.

The Shadow followed me out the door, across the backyard. I half-heartedly tried to outrun him, but I felt him hovering just a half step behind me. I kinda liked his presence, a true shadow. I didn't know where I was running to, but it didn't matter. I wasn't entirely alone.

CHAPTER SIXTEEN

Punching Bag

I only got as far as the dried-up creek. Andrew stopped me dead in my tracks.

"Get outta my way. I wanna go to the Joint."

"That's not a good idea."

"You're not the boss of me!"

"I can't let you go there, at least not until the railing is done."

"I HATE YOU!"

"Then hit me," he challenged. My ears felt like they were about to burn off.

"HIT ME! I can take it," he prodded me again.

I threw a right hook into the dead center of his gut, and he received it like a champ, tightening his muscles. My fist bounced.

"Is that all you got? C'mon. HIT ME!"

I hit again, and my fist bounced again.

"Keep 'em coming. HIT ME, SISTER!"

And my fists took over.

My hands went flying, uncontrollably, beating on Andrew like a punching bag. He kept egging me on, asking for it. After a series of punches, I couldn't remember what I was mad about, I just kept hitting. Sometimes my closed fists went into his gut, other times my fingernails scratched at his arms, and once or twice I sent an open-hand slap to his leg or ribs, only because I couldn't reach his face. He just took it, absorbing every punch.

"HIT ME!" he pointed to his gut, and I punched.

"HIT ME!" he pointed to his ribs, and I punched.

"HIT ME!" he slapped both hands on his chest, and I punched, three times.

"HIT ME!" he opened his arms, exposing his whole body for me to pummel. I hit him some more.

I hit him for the time he tied my hair in a knot behind the headrest in the car. I hit him for the time he tickled me until I peed my pants. I hit him for the time he held me down, spit in my face, and sucked it back up.

When I hesitated a bit between hits, he cocked his head sideways at me and smiled, chidingly.

"C'mon baby sister. You got more in you!"

I punched his left bicep.

"C'mon! Hit me in the face! MOM hits harder than you."

I looked up at his face. He was pointing to his chin. I wanted to, but I didn't think I should, or even could. And yet, I was too delirious to care.

I still can't believe what he did next, or what I did after that.

He spit at me.

Somehow, I dodged it.

Most of it flew over my left shoulder.

I responded with a full-force open-palm right-hand slap across his left cheek.

"Holy SHIT!" his left hand cradled his left cheek, which was instantly red.

I spit in his face.

"Now that's what I'm talking about! Let me have it Sister!"

I punched him, a left jab to the ribs. And then a right jab. And left. Right. Left. Right. My forehead was planted on his chest, and my arms just kept swinging.

He wrapped his arms around me in a big bear hug, restricting my elbows from pulling back for more punches, so I stomped on his foot, then his other foot. He hugged me tighter and lifted me up off the ground so I couldn't kick or hit. I writhed.

He just held me.

Firm.

"That's it. Let it all out." His voice turned to a whisper, almost a coo. "Be mad, sister. You can be as mad as you want."

"I still love you," he whispered.

I paused.

He'd never said that to me before.

Then the hotness got even hotter.

I flailed my legs.

"Andrew loves ya," he whispered in his best Rocky Balboa voice.

I scratched at his ribs.

"I love you, Alex," he whispered again.

I continued to flail.

He held me until I exhausted myself.

I surrendered, limp and heavy in his arms.

And he kept holding me.

We both collapsed to our knees. We sat there in the dry creek bed, his arms wrapped around me, my face pressed to his chest, panting until our breath matched pace. A thousand pounds of fight were left in me, but I had no more reason left to fight.

I felt all sealed up, contained.

Sometime later, we silently got up.

Andrew headed out to the Joint.

I went back to the house.

Mom had cleaned up the kitchen from my oatmeal tantrum, smoothed out the question tree, and placed it on the fridge. She had cleared everything else off the fridge. My question tree was alone behind one simple magnet, and she sat quietly at the table gazing at it while drinking a fresh cup of tea.

"I'm sorry I had a tantrum."

"No sorrys needed, sweetheart. You're meeting Grief for the first time. He can be quite scary."

"Him?"

"Grief. He can be very scary."

Was she talking about the Shadow?

"You've seen him?" I asked, gulping at my words.

She nodded.

"He doesn't have to be scary, you know," she said, pulling out my chair.

"I know," I said, pulling the box of Life cereal down from the cabinet.

"I know you know."

We sat at the table in silence the whole time I ate. She sipped her tea and stared at the question tree.

"Do you wanna talk about it now?" she asked after I had slurped the last of the sugary milk from the bottom of the bowl.

"Not yet." I put my cereal bowl and spoon in the sink.

"You take all the time you need." She took the sponge out of my hand at the kitchen sink. "I'll do your dishes."

I sat down at her place at the table and finished off her tea.

"You can frame it if you want," I said, looking carefully for her response. She paused. Water ran from the faucet over her empty hands.

"Really?" She turned from the kitchen sink. Her eyes were red, puffy.

I was so wrapped up in the cold, thorny blanket of my own pain, I hadn't noticed that Mom hurt too. A lot. For the first time in my life, I saw her as not just my mother, but as someone with flaws and feelings and pain just like mine.

"Yeah. Frame it," I said. She turned off the water and hugged me from above and kissed my head. I felt a wet tear fall and dampen the top of my head.

CHAPTER SEVENTEEN

The Poked Bear

Later that same day, just one day after Teddy died, I heard something from my bedroom window I'd never heard before—Mrs. James yelling. Given that it was the middle of July, and we didn't have air-conditioning, all the windows of our house were open. In all the years we kids had done naughty things, Mrs. James had never once raised her voice with us. In fact, her most stern you'd-better-listen-to-me-or-else-suffer-the-consequences-voice was a tone just barely louder than a whisper.

I ran to the front window of my parents' bedroom and looked through the yellow curtains to the street below. Mr. James had driven up in his BMW, and Mrs. James screamed at him from the end of the driveway.

"YOU AREN'T WELCOME HERE!"

She poked the bear.

The bear got out of the car, slammed the door and marched toward her.

"YOU CAN'T KICK ME OUT, WOMAN, I OWN THIS HOUSE, AND EVERYTHING IN IT! AND IF YOU THINK

YOU ARE GONNA KEEP MY SON FROM ME, YOU'VE GOT ANOTHER THINK COMING."

The Angry Man.

"TEDDY IS DEAD BECAUSE OF YOU," Mrs. James yelled again. "YOU REALLY THINK I BELIEVE ALL THOSE ACCIDENTS WERE JUST ACCIDENTS?! I KNOW YOU HURT HIM!"

Oh, Teddy. What else did he do to you?

"DO YOU THINK I PUSHED HIM?!"

Oh NO! Could he have?

"YOU MIGHT AS WELL HAVE PUSHED HIM!" she screamed as she turned and walked toward the front porch of their house.

Did Mr. James push Teddy?

"I FORBADE HIM FROM GOING UP THERE, I WAS TRYING TO PROTECT HIM!" Mr. James followed her. "HE DISOBEYED ME!"

Mr. James was the bear.

"And keep your voice down, bitch."

"OH REALLY?! YOU'RE ASHAMED TO LET THE NEIGHBORS KNOW WHO AND WHAT YOU ARE, YOU MONSTER! NEWS FLASH, THEY ALREADY KNOW!"

"YOU FUCKING WHORE!" Mr. James slapped her so hard she stumbled backwards and fell off the porch onto the front sidewalk.

Mrs. James!

Before she could get up, he kicked her in the belly. Hard. She screeched the ugliest sound I had ever heard, part hiccup, part burp, part groan. She curled up in the fetal position on her side, clutching her belly. He kicked again. And again. I felt every blow as if he were beating me. With the wind knocked out of me, clutching my own stomach, I picked up the phone on my dad's nightside table and dialed 9-1-1. My Dad ran toward them from our garage with Dave and Andrew not far behind him. It took all three of them to restrain Mr. James while Mom ran to Mrs. James's aid.

"9-1-1 what's your emergency?"

"He's beating her," I choked through my own gulping voice.

"What address?"

I don't remember exactly what I told the woman on the phone. I just remember it seemed like I was on the phone for a long time. Long enough to see Mr. James kick Andrew in the leg and punch Dad in the face. Long enough to see him run back to his car and speed away. Long enough for Dave to run back in the house and pick up the kitchen phone and hear that I was already talking to 9-1-1. Long enough for Dad to carry Mrs. James to the front porch.

I finally hung up when two police cars and an ambulance came speeding down the street for the second day in a row. I walked to the corner of the James's front porch and sat there quietly. I put on my invisibility cloak as the Shadow, Grief, sat down next to me. No one noticed me.

As the paramedics tended to Dad and Mrs. James, Mom spoke to the cop, the same cop who had come yesterday for Teddy's death. This time, Mom quivered as Dave held her, sitting on the porch swing. Andrew paced the length of the porch, ranting, too angry to be coherent.

When I saw that a second police officer had finally stopped talking on the CB radio in the car, I got up from my hiding-in-plain-sight corner. Grief skulked off into the woods. I walked over to the officer, one I recognized as a first responder on the scene for Teddy.

"Hi," I said, shyly.

"Are you okay?"

"Yeah."

A third officer, one I didn't recognize, a woman, got out of the second police car and walked over to us.

"I'll take it from here," she said, and he took a step back.

"It's Alex, right?"

"Yeah."

"You're the one who called 9-1-1, right?"

I nodded.

She looked up at the porch at my mom, who nodded to her.

"Would you be more comfortable if we sat in the car?" she asked.

I nodded.

She looked at my mom again, who once again nodded to her.

I followed her to the squad car. She let me in the passenger side and walked around to the driver's side. When she shut the door from the outside world, the quiet of the car felt comforting, like Grief's silencing cloak. I felt Grief's soothing presence in the back seat.

Are police cars soundproof?

"We don't really need these anymore," she said, turning off the flashing lights, and I felt even calmer. My shining slowly zipped itself back up.

"You've had quite a couple of days," she said calmly.

I nodded.

"Do you want to tell me about it?" she wasn't looking at me. Instead, we both looked out the passenger side window at nothing that mattered.

I nodded.

"Take your time." She turned her body toward me, and put her hand on the back of the seat behind my left shoulder. But somehow I could feel it as if her hand were resting on my shoulder blade. I felt her eyes, too. They weren't on me, which felt nice. I could tell that she just kept looking out the passenger side window like I was.

"You don't have to tell me anything you don't want to."

"Okay."

She took a long, slow breath.

I did the same.

We sat there in silence for several minutes.

And then, I felt the urge to speak.

And I mean really speak.

"I saw it all . . ."

I talked like I didn't need to breathe between sentences. I talked without giving her a chance to ask questions. I spilled specifics out of the recessed corners of my memory that I hadn't even written in my journals. I told her how we were all more than a little scared of Mr. James and had to be careful not to mess anything up when he was around. I listed all of Teddy's major injuries going back to kindergarten. I told her that Teddy was scared, more scared than I had ever seen him. I told her about Angry Man and how terrified Teddy was when he told me that he poked the bear. I told her about Murphy's death, and the Mackey dogs and how they were all stacked up neatly. And I told her details I hadn't remembered before, like the fact that the Mackey dogs' paws were bloody and raw like they had been sliced over and over with razor blades. I told her about Teddy's insomnia and his paper route and morning walks and late night ventures. I described his black eye swollen shut and his fat lip.

The only thing I didn't tell her was about the skinned rabbit.

And the whole time, we just both looked blindly out the passenger side window. She didn't take notes. She didn't turn on a tape recorder. She just listened.

And I felt better.

CHAPTER EIGHTEEN

Friendly Ghosts

The next morning, only two days after Teddy died (it felt like a month had passed) I didn't know what to do with myself.

Kevin and his family were still at their family cabin. Tommy had gone to stay with his aunt in the Twin Cities. Mom was on the phone. Dad went with Dave and Andrew to finish the railing at the Joint. Mrs. James, having spent the night in our guest bedroom, sat on the swing on our front porch.

I plopped myself back in my hiding-in-plain-sight-place on the corner of the porch. I put on my invisibility cloak. I sat in the nothingness of nowhere-ville. My unzipped back pressed up against the corner of the house, one foot out long in front of me, the other foot dangling over the edge of the porch. I just listened to the wind chimes and felt the warmth of the sun on my face.

Once in a while, I'd gaze at Mrs. James as she rocked herself, staring off into space. Her eyes were different than I'd ever seen before, somehow both vacant and full at the same time. She either didn't notice me there or didn't mind. The rhythmic squeak from the porch swing chain against the ceiling hook blended nicely with the irregular bells of the wind chimes. Together, they sounded like a melancholic lullaby. We passed the time together, yet apart; not sleeping, but not entirely awake either; wanting to be alone, but not entirely alone.

"Alex?" Mrs. James spoke with a sleepy voice, "How long have you been there?"

I shrugged my shoulders.

Time was irrelevant.

She patted the seat of the porch swing next to her.

She looked at me with Teddy's eyes.

We walk . . . we don't talk.

We swing . . . we don't speak.

So I sat down next to her, my legs not quite long enough to touch the floor from the hanging edge of the porch seat. The echoing emptiness of the gap in the back of my heart, my unzipping, fit perfectly between the slats on the back of the porch swing.

"Thanks for being here," she whispered.

I nodded.

A while later, she scooted herself down on the swing just enough to lay her head on my shoulder. Eventually, she tucked her feet up underneath her and laid her head in my lap. The porch swing slowly stopped swinging, the metronomic squeak silenced, leaving us with just the occasional breeze and chime.

With her head in my lap, she cried a quiet whimper. Slow tears oozed onto my leg. Neither of us made any effort to wipe them away. Every once in a while, she took in a heavy gasp, followed by a dense sigh. I was all out of tears. Besides, she had enough for both of us that day.

Grief stood behind us, occasionally pushing the swing ever so gently with a soft breeze. His knotty-knuckled hand reached in between the slats of the porch swing and stroked the back of my heart with the same tenderness I used to stroke Mrs. James's hair.

Sometime later, Mom came out and sat down on the Adirondack chair opposite the swing.

"Alice?" she said softly.

Mrs. James sat up, planting her feet on the floor, stopping the swing.

"We can go," Mom said.

"Now?"

"Yes, now. Do you think you can do that? Otherwise, I can schedule another time."

"No. I wanna go now." She took a deep breath. "I need to."

"Where are you going?" I asked.

"Mrs. James needs to speak with a lawyer. I got her an appointment."

"You'll go with me?" Mrs. James pleaded with my mom.

"Of course."

Then Mom looked at me.

"Will you be okay? I can go get Dad to be with you."

"No. I'll be fine."

I went for a bike ride. When I got back to our block, all the neighborhood cars were gone, except Freaky Mr. Weismann's beat-up old green hearse, the one he used as a construction truck.

Freaky Mr. Weismann.

Why did we even call him that?

Mr. Weismann always smiled at us and was careful to drive slow when we were riding our bikes. He even parked farther away from his house whenever we were playing soccer or hockey in the street. At Halloween he always gave out the full-sized candy bars, two each, knowing which was each of our favorites. Almond Joy for Tommy. Mars for Teddy. Three Musketeers AND Milky Way for Kevin. And Snickers for me. But he rarely spoke. He'd always nod or smile. When he did speak, it was always in a low, humble tone, and with very few words.

When I got back from the library, Mr. Weismann's garage door was open. I'd never seen the inside of his garage before. He kept his hearse in the driveway, and always entered his house through the front door, or the service door on the side of the garage. I guess I just thought it was broken, or that his garage was so full of stuff that he couldn't open it. But there it was, open, for all to see. What surprised me was that it was immaculately clean and perfectly organized.

He was inside, sitting on the ground, his legs out long in a V-shape, with an old rusty coffee can full of nuts and bolts and screws in front of him. He looked like a toddler in a grown-up body, with his chubby baby-fat legs sticking out from ratty cargo shorts. His too-big sausage-like fingers worked at sorting the nuts and bolts and screws into a number of tiny drawers pulled out from a brand new toolbox. His fingers fumbled with the tiny objects, unable to separate the tiny bolts attached to the wrong-sized nuts, often dropping the wrong screw into the wrong drawer and struggling to pull it back out. Although he dropped the wrong item into the wrong drawer almost as often as he hit his target, he worked with such patience with himself. First he would try to fish out the wrong item with the puffy ends of his fingers, and if that didn't work, he'd pour the contents out into the palm of his hand. He worked meticulously, patiently, as if he was enjoying the simplicity of the task. He was so focused on his work, I wondered if he knew I was standing in his driveway watching. I wondered how long I had been watching him. Time is irrelevant.

"Can I help you with that?" I offered.

"I was wondering how long it might be before you offered," he said, revealing that he knew I had been there the whole time.

I sat down cross-legged in front of the rusty coffee can while he rolled over to his side to push himself up onto all fours and eventually stand up. Then he pulled three more coffee cans off a shelf and placed them next to me. In just a couple minutes, my brain memorized which pieces went to which drawers, and I was working like a fast paced automatic machine.

"You're good at that," he said as he sat back down on the ground in the same position he was before, this time with a greasy old socket wrench set between his knees. He pulled a worn red bandana from his back pocket and started cleaning each socket by stuffing the corners of the bandana into the sockets. We worked together in silence for several minutes before I found the courage to speak again.

"Um, Mr. Weismann? Can I ask you a question?"

"Yes Alex, you may." I appreciated both his gentle use of my name, and his subtle correction of my grammar. I made a mental note to myself, to be more careful with my word choices.

"Mr. Weismann, *may* I ask you a question?"

"Of course." He smiled kindly at me, and I wondered again why we always referred to him as Freaky Mr. Weismann. He wasn't freaky at all, but rather very kind.

"Why do you drive a beat-up old green hearse?"

"Bessie!" His voice had a happy giggle inside it. He carefully placed the socket he was working on back in its nesting space in the box with the others, and then worked his way back to standing.

"Allow me to introduce you to her!" he said, digging in his pocket for keys with one hand while offering his other hand to help me up from the ground.

I knew what the coffin compartment looked like. We all did. Mr. Weismann had remodeled to use as a construction bed with tools, tool boxes, and space for lumber and supplies. But I'd never seen the driver's cabin, which had dark tinted windows. I was more than curious to know what it looked like.

"Bessie? You named your hearse Bessie?"

"My father named her Bessie. He owned a funeral home in the Twin Cities. Bessie was the name of the very first person he buried. When my pop died just before I moved in here, I couldn't get myself to get rid of her. So I transformed her into my utility truck," he said, unlocking the passenger side door and opening it for me. I sat down, and he left the door open as he walked around to the driver's side.

The seats were a plush-but-worn green velvet with several multicolored patches sewn in to repair various holes and tears. A heavy, black, velvet curtain lined the back wall partition between the front seat cabin and coffin compartment. Old black & white pictures of various people wallpapered the ceiling.

He turned on the car without starting the engine so that the music began to play. Dean Martin's voice crooned from a cassette tape plugged into an outdated stereo system. He turned up the volume so loud I was glad that he had left the doors open, and he started singing along with a deep, rich voice as melodic as Frank Sinatra. *Who knew Mr. Weismann could sing?* He was so consumed by the song and his singing, I didn't dare interrupt him. When the song was over, he reached up and touched one of the pictures pinned to the ceiling of the hearse.

"Thanks, Aunt Becky. I needed that one," he said, and he busted out laughing a deep belly laugh that shook the bench seat beneath us.

"Singing in the car gives me such joy," he said as he turned down the music to a level where we could comfortably talk over it. "Bessie is my happy place. No matter how bad a day I have, Bessie can always cheer me up. And, all my favorite people are in here with me."

He gestured to the collage of photos on the ceiling.

"Who are they?" I asked.

"This one is my pop. He loved Bessie more than I do."

"This here is my mum," he said with a British accent, pointing to an older and ratty photo of a young woman in the 1940s. "She was from England, and she died when she gave birth to me."

One by one, I pointed to pictures.

A friend who died in Vietnam.

An uncle who went down in a fighter jet in WWII.

His grandparents.

His great aunt.

His father-in-law.

All deceased.

After naming each picture, he would take a moment to take a breath. He looked almost as though in that breath-moment he was calling that person and waiting for them to sit down between us. Then he'd tell me some little tidbit about them or recall a short memory. His stories were all of people he loved who had died. While I felt like the stories should be sad, they weren't. None of them were. I enjoyed his stories, and the fact that I didn't have to talk. I liked listening.

"I'm sorry. I must be boring you with all these memories of dead people," he said when we'd gotten through about half the pictures on the ceiling.

"No. Not at all. Can I meet them all?"

And so we continued.

I expected my unzipping to open, but it didn't. Rather, I felt a warmth on my back, like a hand resting on the unzipping place. I even turned around to touch the seat of the car to see if there was a heating pad there. But there was nothing.

After I'd pointed to the last picture (save the one hiding behind the driver's side sun visor), the music stopped. Once again, Mr. Weismann exploded into a short fit of belly laughter.

"That was a classic Casper moment, the music stopping exactly when I finished my introductions."

"A Casper moment? Like Casper the Friendly Ghost?"

"Precisely. There is such a thing as friendly ghosts, like Casper, and they are the best kind of ghosts because they give us the best surprises."

"All of these are your friendly ghosts?"

"Yes, and I have more. There's not enough room on this ceiling for all of them."

"Can Teddy be one of my friendly ghosts now?"

"Of course he can, Alex. If you invite him to be part of your congress of ghosts, he will be one of your friendly ghosts who gives you the kind of surprises you never see coming."

"What do you mean by a 'congress of ghosts'?" I asked.

"Like a herd of cattle, or murder of crows, or a school of fish, or a pack of wolves."

"A group of ghosts is called a congress?"

"Yeah. They govern the spiritual laws of the universe."

"I like that."

"I also have a tizzy of fairies that live amongst my flower beds." He pointed to the various multicolored garden ornaments peeking from behind the day lilies and rose bushes.

"Oh! I love those!"

"And my host of angels," he said, pointing to the blue bottles dangling from the limbs of his trees.

"And my pleasure of pixies who play my wind chimes."

"A congress of ghosts, a host of angels, a tizzy of fairies, and a pleasure of pixies." I listed each one out loud, making a mental note to write them down later. "What about your gnomes?"

"That term is rather pedestrian. It's called a lawn of gnomes."

"Yeah, that's boring."

"Trust me, Alex, gnomes are far from boring. They are as humble as hobbits, but just as witty, with a wicked streak of mischief in them." As he finished his sentence, the cassette tape reached its end and spit itself out of the player.

"I think your gnomes are sticking their tongues out at you," I suggested, pointing to the tape player, which looked like a face. The volume and tuner buttons were eyes, the tape deck the mouth, and the tape was a tongue.

"Another Casper moment." Mr. Weismann laughed, slapping the steering wheel. His hand bounced off the steering wheel and back-handed the sun-visor, causing the one remaining hidden picture to fall into his lap. It was a young girl who couldn't have been more than six years old.

"Mischievous little bastards," he muttered as he flipped the tape over and fed it back into the machine. When Dean Martin started singing *I'll Be Seeing You,* Mr. Weismann's eyes went dark as he stared down at the picture in his lap.

My back unzipped.

CHAPTER NINETEEN

Full of Care

Mr. Weismann dropped his chin to his chest and stopped breathing entirely. A longer-than-comfortable moment later, he choked in a breath, and then sobbed openly. His loud wails sounded almost identical to his belly laughs, and they drowned out Dean Martin entirely. As he sobbed, he grabbed his head in both his hands, and then dragged his hands down to cover his face. By the time his hands dragged off the edge of his chin, he had stopped crying. His breath got slower and deeper, and his hands rested hand over hand on his heart until the song ended.

Then he turned off the stereo and turned to me.

"This is Hannah. My daughter. And her dog Pebbles," he paused, humming along with the music, gazing lovingly at the picture.

"I'm sorry," I whispered.

"Listen to me, Alex. It's is very important in life to be full of care. I don't mean just cautious. I mean FULL, to the brim of your soul, with CARE. I spent too many years of my life being careless. Then, I lost them."

"Them?" I asked.

"Open the glove box," he said pointing to the compartment in front of my knees. I pulled the latch and found the rattiest of all the photographs. A young woman sat on a picnic blanket under a tree, holding a small baby over her shoulder, with a puppy asleep in her lap.

"My wife, Emilyn, our daughter, Hannah, and their dog, Pebbles." He paused for a full breath between each of their names, almost as if he were standing at their graves, introducing me to each one.

"Emilyn died because I was careless. I was too caught up in my work, making enough money and working really long hours. Most nights I wasn't home until well after they were both asleep in bed, and I'd often leave before they woke. I didn't spend enough time with them. I was careless with my time. I was careless with my energy. I didn't notice. I didn't pay attention. Alex, part of being full of care is about paying attention.

"But I don't need to tell *you* that. I have a feeling you pay very close attention, sometimes too close."

How did he know?

"May I ask, how did they die?"

"Alex, that story is not nearly as pretty as the picture you hold in your hands," he said, and paused, looking me right in the eye.

"I can handle it," I said.

"After what you've seen so far this summer, I suspect you can."

He paused again, taking a deep breath, and then sighed.

"Emilyn was a very lonely woman, even before I met her. When we married, she told me that her biggest fear was to be

145

lonely for the rest of her life. I promised her I would never let her be lonely again. We lived out in the country. Emilyn didn't drive, so she was home alone with Hannah all day long."

He paused, fiddling with keys dangling from the ignition.

Then he took another long inhale and sigh.

"Emilyn loved that dog, almost as much as she loved Hannah. The neighbor farm had brought her over, a six-month-old runt of the litter. She was a very cuddly pup, so loving. Emilyn poured everything of herself into our little girl and that pup. But I didn't want a dog, and I was angry that Emilyn had accepted her into our home without talking to me. To me, Pebbles was another mouth to feed who shed fur everywhere. I used to shove her out of the room with my foot, not quite kicking her, but nudging her forcefully. I was careless."

He paused again, turned the key in the ignition to off.

"Hannah was 16, and we had buried Pebbles just a few months earlier. Against Emilyn's wishes, I got Hannah a convertible for her birthday. I thought it would give them both some freedom they didn't have before. I'd hoped it would encourage Emilyn to learn how to drive, so she could get to town and make herself some friends."

He motioned to the glove box again.

"Look inside the operations manual," he said.

I pulled out the ratty book and found another photograph pressed between the pages. Hannah stood proudly in front of a bright red VW Rabbit, the keys dangling from her fingers.

"It was a good car. She named it Bunny. She kept a little bunny charm hanging from the rearview mirror and a bunny ears headband on the dash that she would often wear while she drove with the top down."

He took the first photograph from his lap and placed it gently on the dashboard, and lined up the other two next to it.

"That day when I got home from work, Bunny was parked crooked in the driveway, blocking both stalls of the garage door. When I pulled my truck onto the grass, my headlights lit up the front porch. Hannah sat cross-legged on the floor of the porch with her bunny ears on, crying. When I asked her what was wrong, she just pointed to the door."

He took a long, deep sigh and burst into another 30 seconds of heavy sobs, pulling at his hair and dragging his hands down his face as he had done before.

"She was in the bathtub, blood everywhere. I just stood at the bathroom door, frozen, for I don't know how long. When I went back out to the front porch, Hannah was gone."

He sighed a heavy breath that seemed to deflate his entire body. Then, I noticed my own wetness. Although my vision hadn't been disturbed one bit because the tears just spilled, a steady, soft trickle. We sat there together in silence for several minutes before he spoke again.

"That was the last day I ever saw Hannah, and the last day I was ever careless."

"Where is Hannah now?" I asked in a whisper.

"I have no idea."

"I'm sorry."

"It's okay." He flipped the sun visor down and pressed Hannah's picture back on the sticky residue of double-sided tape on the vanity mirror.

When he flipped the sun visor back up, his gaze locked onto something he saw in the back corner of his garage. It was Grief, in his hooded cloak, partially hidden between the shadows of a stack of two-by-fours.

Does Mr. Weismann see Grief like I do?

"Do you see that?" I nodded my head towards the Shadow in the garage.

"Yes, Alex, I know Grief well."

"What's he look like?"

"I suspect you know the answer to that question."

I nodded.

"You see him now, don't you?" he asked.

"Yes. He's leaning against the two-by-fours. But if I weren't paying attention, I would think he's just an eerie shadow."

"I *knew* you could see!" Mr. Weismann exclaimed, excitedly hitting the top of the steering wheel.

"Where else have you seen him?" he asked.

"He was at the balloon launch at school, when Mrs. Schmidt died."

"Of course he was," he affirmed.

"Where have you seen him?" I asked.

"Grief and I are good buddies. I sometimes wonder if he has taken up residence in our quiet cul de sac because of me," he said.

"I think he is here for everyone," I suggested.

"Such as?" he asked.

"He lurks in Mrs. Tomkins's pantry, whispering in her ear which cookies and cakes to bake whenever she feels worried or sad or scared, which we know is quite often."

"Yes . . . Yes. Where else?"

"He used to skulk around Mr. Mackey's front yard, playing with Whiskey, Bourbon, and Brandy, whenever Mr. Mackey passed out on the lawn overnight. But ever since . . ." I paused to swallow the knot in my throat along with the grotesque memory of Teddy and Murphy finding the Mackey dogs dead in the woods. "Now, he just sits in Mackey's broken lawn chairs," I said.

"He pushes Mrs. James in the porch swing," he added.

"Did you see us earlier?" I asked.

"I did."

"Have you ever talked to him?" I asked.

"Yes Alex. Grief and I talk. We talk every day, several times a day. Ever since I lost my Hannah, I've lived a lonely life. Grief is sometimes my best and only friend."

"Do you sometimes pour him a glass of beer?" I asked, remembering the many times we kids had seen Mr. Weismann sit in one of the two Adirondack chairs on his front porch with a can of beer in his hand and another untouched one sitting on the armrest of the other chair.

"You've noticed that, huh?"

"Uh huh."

"Of course you would notice that."

"He doesn't talk like a human. I can't hear him with my ears. Is it like that for you too?" I asked.

"When you see him, Alex, is it like a shadow that you aren't looking at? That if you look right at him, he disappears, but you see him through the side of your eyes?"

"Yeah," I said.

"For me, talking with him is like that, too. I don't have to talk out loud. I just think a thought. And then, I don't hear him with my ears. It's more like a feeling and a knowing."

I nodded.

"A tingle," he continued, "a zing, a chill, a hot flash, usually followed by a thought somewhere in my mind and I don't know how it got there."

I nodded again. He was describing my unzipping.

"Sometimes it's Grief," he said. "But not always. I have a lot of friends I talk to," he said, pointing to the pictures on his ceiling. "My congress of ghosts."

And then it happened, but different. It started as a tingle all down my arms, then goosebumps on my legs. Finally, it became a thought that crawled up the back of my neck and lodged itself on the back of my tongue.

Ask him.

I swallowed, trying to shove the thought down my throat.

But instead, it inflated, and my tongue felt big.

Ask him.

I swallowed again, opened my mouth, and was stunned at what came out of my mouth.

"How do I invite Teddy to be part of my congress of ghosts?"

Mr. Weismann took a deep breath before he turned in his seat to face his whole body toward me.

"I can't tell you that. I wish I could. What I do know is that you will know, when the time is right."

"Oh," I swallowed again, "okay." I didn't know what to say.

"The Tao says 'loss is not as bad as wanting more.' When you learn to stop wanting more from Teddy, and be grateful for all you did have, that's when Grief will hold your hand instead of squeezing your heart."

"How did you learn to stop wanting more?"

"Alex, I don't think we ever do, completely."

"No. I suppose we can't."

"But Alex, this much I do know. Grief has two faces. Like the comedy and drama faces of theater. Just as tears can be both of sorrow or laughter, Grief can have a sad frown-face, or he can be quite sweet, with a gentle, soft smile. He can also hold both faces in one. Have you ever laugh-cried or cry-laughed?"

"I've laughed so hard I've cried, if that's what you mean."

"Sort of. Have you ever cried so hard that you laugh?"

"No, I don't think I have."

"You will, one day, and that's the day you'll see Grief's two faces at once."

"And the day he can squeeze my heart and hold my hand at the same time."

"Yes, Alex. That's it," he said with a proud glint in his eye. "Welcome to the Grief Club."

"Thanks," I said, and swallowed, "I think."

Several minutes later, we both wiped our faces of the tears and got out of the car without a word. I followed him into the garage and sat back down with the old coffee can of screws and nuts and bolts to sort into the tiny drawers of a new toolbox. He set back to work cleaning the socket wrench set.

Later that night, I rummaged through my bedroom until I found a picture of Teddy I liked. I wrote on the back of the picture:

Teddy James 1973-1985
to be secured to the ceiling of my car one day

CHAPTER TWENTY

Side A - Sad Songs

That next morning, the whole neighborhood went back to work. I packed my backpack with a brand new spiral bound notebook, a pack of colored pencils, a few pens, a sandwich and a couple juice boxes, my Walkman, a spare set of AA batteries, and a handful of pictures of Teddy. In my Walkman was the mixtape Teddy had made for me last Christmas. Then, just as I was about to leave the house, I saw Dad's birdwatching binoculars on the end table. I didn't quite know why, but I tossed those in too. I climbed up to the top of the Stink House, where I listened to that mixtape three times through while filling every single page of the notebook.

I gave myself one rule: write nonstop, no cross-outs, no pausing, just write until I had nothing left to say.

I started by writing a letter to Teddy. It began sweetly, telling him all the great things I loved about him, but then it morphed into anger as I raged at him for leaving me. I filled several pages with anger at him for killing himself. Until I decided he just wouldn't do that. He couldn't. There was no way Teddy committed suicide.

Then I felt bad. I felt really bad, guilty for even thinking Teddy would do that. So I started writing apologies. I apologized for thinking he'd even consider killing himself. I apologized for not paying attention, for not being *full of care* in terms of all of his "accidents" and not DOING anything about it. I apologized to Mr. Weismann for calling him freaky. I apologized to Mrs. James for the time we left the frogs and toads in the bathtub. I apologized to my mom for crumpling up the question tree. And then, I apologized to Teddy for getting mad when he didn't give me my Christmas present until two weeks after New Year's because he was saving money to buy the latest Prince album for the mixtape I was listening to.

Loss is not as bad as wanting more.

Mr. Weismann's words from the Tao filled my head like smoke trapped in a glass. I wrote about all the more I wanted from Teddy. I started each line with "I wish . . ." I wrote about wanting Teddy to be the one to give me my first kiss. I wrote about wanting to get our driver's licenses and go joyriding together. I wrote about wanting to graduate high school with him. I wrote about wanting his help picking a college because we both knew Kevin and Tommy's advice would be useless.

Then, I wrote about all that I did get with Teddy. I started each line with "I'm grateful for . . ." and filled three times as many pages as the "I wishes." As I wrote, the words burned the memories deeper into the inside of my skull, tattoos matching the worm question squiggles. The memories spilled out of me in sloppy, fast handwriting; big, playful looping letters, forming pictures on the page.

When the memories slowed to a trickle, I turned to a new page, writing across the top in big block bold letters.

HE'S IN A BETTER PLACE NOW

And then I broke my own rule, and I crossed it out, several times. It was a bullshit line that people say at funerals that doesn't make anyone feel any better. It's crap. I wrote underneath it "There's no such thing as a better place. And Teddy would've said so."

In slow, stuttered handwriting, I wrote about all the injustices he suffered in his life. I thought to myself that this could only be one page. So when I ran out of room, I just kept writing new sentences over the old ones, layering words and phrases on top of each other until everything was completely unintelligible. I wrote about all the things in life he didn't have to endure anymore, and all the things he got to skip because he won the lottery of an early grave. I couldn't write those things quickly enough. They dribbled in bits and burps, sometimes fierce angry letters, and other times almost whispers on the page. I wrote about how I hated the Angry Man, Mr. James, and how I blamed him for Teddy's death. Even if the cops came back and ruled Teddy's death either a suicide or accident, I knew, I just KNEW that Mr. James was the real killer. How I wished they could find proof that he'd pushed Teddy, and they could put him away forever. I didn't want anyone to ever be able to decipher what I wrote on this page, and when I ran out of burps and spits and fizzles, I put down the pen, massaged my writing hand with my other hand and gazed at a page filled with words on top of words on top of words, a squiggly cloud of madness.

Then I turned the page and ripped out the next page, which had flecks and specks that bled through. I crumpled it up and shoved it into the side pocket of my backpack. Leaving my pen as a bookmark in the notebook, I stood up and walked several laps around the tiny roof of the Stink House. It took me three times clockwise, three times counterclockwise, and twice again clockwise before I felt calm enough to sit back down and write some more.

I flipped the mixtape back to side A in my Walkman once again. I pulled out the handwritten insert and read what Teddy had written to me.

As I listened, that fourth time through, I paused the tape between each song, rewound and listened again, and paused again to write about the song. Each song got its own page in the notebook. I started each page with the words Teddy had written to me, and then wrote him my response.

Side A - Sad Songs

Sad Songs Say So Much - Elton John
because sometimes you just gotta let yourself be sad

Teddy, I hurt. I just hurt.
This hurts more than I ever knew hurting could hurt. I think about how it must've felt for you to fall onto Excalibur. I don't know what is worse, imagining it and not knowing how it felt, or what it feels like to see it. You didn't have to see it, Teddy. You didn't have to see yourself hanging there above me like a dead angel. This kind of hurt, I don't know if it can ever go away. All hope IS gone. So I'm turning on the sad songs.

When Doves Cry - Prince
doves crying is the ultimate of sad

You loved this song, you called it beautiful genius. Well, now this dove you know named Alex, she is crying. I can't ever forget the picture of you kissing me that night under the Joint. How can you leave me here standing in the cold world? Dammit, Teddy, why didn't I ever tell you about those butterflies I had for you? Why didn't I ever let you know? Writing to you now, it's just not enough. I'm just standing here alone, a crying dove, talking to the wind, alone in this world, so cold without you.

Time After Time - Cyndi Lauper
I don't know if time heals all wounds, but I hope so

You were always telling me to go slow.
Now I get it.
I wanna get an old-fashioned suitcase and fill it with all the things that are you. I wanna find a clock with a second hand, the kind you can wind and unwind, and keep it with your pictures and things to remind me to go slow. You can't be full of care unless you go slow. Oh my God, Teddy, were you friends with Mr. Weismann?! Did he teach you about being full of care? Did you know him like I know him now? Why didn't you tell me?

Missing You - John Waite
I played this song the whole time you were at camp last summer, trying to pretend I didn't miss you, but I did miss you, terribly.

I can't catch my breath. My heart is frozen since you died.

Dammit, Teddy, there's no long-distance line for this kind of missing you. I can't pretend I'm not missing you. I'll miss you every day for the rest of my life.

Speaking of, why didn't you tell me how you felt about me?! Oh wait, because you DID! In this mixtape that took you extra long to make at Christmas. How was I so dense? How could I be so dumb? How come I never figured it out? Oh Teddy, now I'll never get to tell you that I felt the same way.

Against All Odds - Phil Collins
This is the ultimate of all sad love songs - EVER!

You're right, Teddy, this is the ultimate of all sad love songs, EVER. How can you just leave me? I didn't even get to watch you leave.

The empty space is unbearable. There's so much I need to tell you. So many things I never said. And now all I have is this empty space and my tears. You're the only one who ever knew me, really knew me, Teddy.

How am I supposed to go on without you?

CHAPTER TWENTY-ONE

The Mood Ring

Grief has two faces.

Side B was the happy side.

Even though I'd already heard it three times, I hadn't really been paying attention. I didn't think I could listen to the happy songs and pay attention, much less write about them. I needed to let myself be sad a little longer.

I packed up my backpack and climbed back down to find something else to do, anything else. Just as I got to the James's driveway, a police car came down the hill. The neighborhood was still quiet. I was quite sure I was the only one around.

It was the woman cop, the same one who listened to my whole story.

"Hi, Alex," she said, getting out of the car with a stapled-shut brown paper bag the size of a grocery bag. "Is Mrs. James around?"

"No. She and Tommy are staying with her sister in the Twin Cities, I think," I said.

"Oh," she said, putting the paper bag back in the squad car. "I forgot she told us she would be going there. I'll contact her there."

"May I ask you a question?" I said, not wanting her to leave.

"Sure." She closed the squad car and turned around to face me, giving me her full attention. In that moment I understood why I had felt so comfortable talking to her. She was full of care.

"Did Mr. James kill Teddy?" I asked, fiddling with the zipper on my backpack.

"No, Alex," she said, using my name just like Mr. Weismann did. It was comforting. "He had a solid alibi," she said while reaching for my hand to stop my fiddling. "But you don't need to worry about him anymore. He's in custody on domestic assault charges."

"Will I have to testify?"

"No, Mr. James is negotiating a plea bargain," she continued. "It's my hope that you will never have to see him ever again."

"Oh. Okay," I said. The words stuck in my throat.

The officer put her hand on the squad car door as if to open it, but then she paused.

She took a deep breath.

And another one.

I waited.

Finally, she opened the door, reached in, and opened the brown paper bag, pulling apart the staples. I watched carefully, curious about what she had that was Teddy's, wishing she would just leave the whole bag with me. Thinking I would put it all in an old-fashioned suitcase.

She pulled out several items, each sealed in a Ziploc bag.

A pair of binoculars.

The cut-off shorts Teddy was wearing when he fell.

Teddy's Walkman.

A copy of the same mixtape Teddy had given me.

The last bag she pulled out, the smallest of them all, she kept in her hand as she replaced the other contents back in the bag. I couldn't see what was in it.

Then she closed the squad car and turned back to me.

"Are you doing okay?"

"Yeah. It's hard." I paused and choked back another tear. "But I'll be okay."

"I know you will," she said, as if there were more to the sentence, but she paused again, this time even longer than before.

A true awkward silence.

She just stood there, not getting back in her car, and not looking at me, just staring at her hand and the plastic bag she clutched in it. Finally, she reached her empty hand out to me, palm up, inviting my hand to hers.

When I gave her my hand, she turned my hand palm up and placed the plastic bag on top, leaving her other hand on top while she spoke.

"I was supposed to give this to Mrs. James. I'm not supposed to do this." She paused, another awkward silence. "But I'm giving it to you. It was meant for you."

She looked at me for acknowledgement.

I'll never speak of this ever, to anyone, I said to her with my eyes, but my mouth never opened. I just nodded at her. We had a silent conversation. Somehow I understood that she wasn't telling me not to tell anyone. Rather, she was telling me that what she was giving me was very, very important for me to have.

"We found this up in the tree fort, the one you call the Joint, with a number of other things Teddy had with him."

She squeezed my hand in hers.

"I understand Teddy died on your birthday. This was a wrapped gift that had your name on it. In order to process it as evidence, we had to unwrap it."

She released my hand, leaving the plastic bag in it.

"You can open it. It's yours to keep," she said.

I pulled open the seal. It was a mood ring, and not a cheap one. Sterling silver, one I had picked out of a catalog months ago. If memory served, it was around $50, which to a 13-year-old kid in 1985 was a lot of money. It wasn't one of those adjustable rings, it was sized precisely to fit my more-slender-than-average finger.

I pulled it out and put it on. It was a perfect fit.

Electric tingles zapped from my finger up my arm to my shoulder, and chicken skin appeared on both my arms. The zingers tripped my heartbeat until I felt it *th-thump* in my lips.

Flash of memory.

Teddy's lips on mine.

"Thank you," I mumbled, barely a whisper.

"That's a very special gift," she said.

"It's beautiful," I whispered.

Another awkward silence.

"Do you still have my business card, Alex?"

I nodded.

"You can use that number anytime you want," she said, placing her hand on my shoulder. "Not just if you think of something more about the case. You call me about anything, you hear?"

I nodded again.

"You take care of yourself, Alex."

"I will."

As she got back in the car and drove away, I twisted the mood ring on my finger. Its stone had turned a brilliant, deep indigo blue. I opened the tiny pamphlet that came with the ring and read the color chart as Mr. Weismann's voice echoed in my head.

There is such a thing as friendly ghosts, like Casper, and they are the best kind of ghosts because they give us the best surprises.

Indigo blue meant peace.

The Tao says "loss is not as bad as wanting more." When you learn to stop wanting more from Teddy, and be grateful for all you did have, that's when Grief will hold your hand instead of squeezing your heart.

A Casper moment. My back unzipped and my shining electrified all the way down into my legs.

How do I invite Teddy to be part of my congress of ghosts?

I can't tell you that. I wish I could. What I do know is that you will know, when the time is right.

I started running, as fast as I could, my backpack bouncing heavily on my shoulders. I needed to get to the tree fort.

Have you ever laugh-cried or cry-laughed?

I didn't know why I had to go, or what I would do there, but I knew once I got there I would know.

CHAPTER TWENTY-TWO

The Ancient One

When I got there, I dropped my backpack at my feet.

The ancient oak gazed down at me.

All the other times I had been there, I had been so focused on the tree fort that I had never really looked at the tree itself. The tree was no longer just the ugly old oak tree that had been struck by lightning. It had a whole new energy, a personality. She was an ancient, wise, living, breathing being.

Taking her in completely overwhelmed me. So, I focused in on her trunk. The knots and twists of her bark looked almost like flames.

And then, I knew what I had to do.

I gathered stones from the dried-up creek bed and built a heart-shaped fire pit in the space between the tree and the stump that was once Excalibur. I built a tiny teepee of kindling and dried leaves.

When I pulled my spiral notebook out of my backpack to rip out a few empty pages to start the fire, a magnifying glass dropped from between the pages. It was the size of a quarter, a Cracker Jack prize that had long been lost in the bottom of my backpack.

"Thanks, Teddy," I said out loud, shoving the magnifying glass deep in my pocket.

Hoping my friendly ghost might have more surprises for me, I dumped out all the contents of my backpack. In the side pocket, I discovered a handful of smooth stones Teddy had brought me back from his family trip to Lake Superior last summer. In the front pocket, I found two empty granola bar wrappers and an embroidery floss friendship bracelet, the last of many I had made for the sixth-grade Christmas Bazaar fundraiser. And in one of the pen slots, I found my Honeywell Swiss Army knife.

One by one, I arranged the pictures of Teddy onto Excalibur's stump, anchoring each one with a smooth stone. I used the Swiss Army knife to carve Teddy's name into the stump. I carefully placed the friendship bracelet to underline Teddy's name. When I felt like there was nothing else to add, I put my binoculars and Walkman back into the backpack, zipped it up, and left it at the base of the tree fort ladder before turning my attention back to my fire.

I sat cross-legged this time in front of the fire pit, positioned at an angle so I could see both the tree and Teddy's shrine. I ripped out two pages, tore them in half and in half again, crumpled them up, and strategically placed them inside the kindling teepee. I dug the magnifying glass out of my pocket, steadied my elbow on my leg and pointed the spotlight directly on the paper inside the teepee.

C'mon Teddy. Help me out here.

After about a minute, one very long minute, the paper started to smoke, and then smolder. And the tiniest gentle breeze fluttered my hair into my face. And just like that, a flame! And the flame grew. I fed it some leaves, and then a couple twigs, and within a few minutes, I had a full fire.

One piece at a time, I ripped the pages from the notebook, crumpled them up and fed them to the fire. Occasionally I added enough twigs and leaves to keep the fire going at a steady, controllable burn. I lost time as I read my own words and watched them burn.

> The world around me is turning too quickly now, Teddy.
> When I said I wanted to grow up, I didn't mean like this.
> Life isn't about making words out of the alphabet letters in the spoon anymore. The world of adulthood is a chunky noodle soup with Brussel sprouts that I have to chew and swallow like a grown-up, even if it makes me gag.
> How did you die, Teddy?
> Why did you have to die?
> Who's gonna be my best friend now?

The whole time, through every burning, scribbled page of my notebook, Grief stood behind me, holding me, while at the same time, giving me space. I didn't cry. Not even when I lit the last page and watched charred bits of ash floating up to the sky. The heat of the flames licked away my tears before they could fully form on my face until there were no more flames.

As the last bit of fire extinguished, I felt this urge, this strange and compelling urge. I took off my shoes and socks and walked around the inside of the heart-shaped fire pit, as if I were stomping out the already-extinguished fire. The earth was warm, but not too hot. It was comforting.

But that wasn't enough.

I sat inside the heart-shaped fire pit, like a toddler splashing in a kiddie pool, and played in the warm-but-not-too-hot earth. I gathered the soil and ash from the fire pit and rubbed it into the soles of my feet, the palms of my hands, my legs, my arms, and even my face.

Then I looked up.

At her.

Her roots grew both wide and deep. I felt them holding me, more than just gravity, like tentacles with suction cups. Not like a scary octopus, but in a good way, like loving Mother Earth arms, holding me to her.

The patterns in the bark of her trunk were no longer flames, but folds of her dress. A face with an ever-so-subtle smile. Her largest and lowest branches spread out into welcoming arms rising up above her face.

Her shimmering leaves flickered in the breeze, glistening silver, catching and reflecting rays of sunlight like a glittering heartbeat. They rained pixie dust from their tips onto the roof of the tree fort, where two sets of small wind chimes dangled, singing like Tinker Bell fairies.

I felt the Shadow's cold hand on the middle of my back, my back heart space. And then, his cloaked density next to me. This visit was different than all the times before.

She's quite a presence, isn't she? he said.

"Uh huh." I could barely speak, I was in such awe.

Look. He pointed up.

Just above the angled peak of the tree fort roof, the string of one deflated purple balloon twisted its way up a branch. One of my

13 wishes stared down at me, taunting me from its place near the sky.

You wished for this, Alex. Which makes you so very special, because very few wish this wish. And even fewer are capable of receiving that kind of wish.

A light breeze blew, and the tree's pixie dust rained on us like a glittery mist. I felt the bells of the wind chimes plucking at the tiny strings inside the marrow of my bones. My heart started beating heavier, so densely that I could feel it pulse in my fingertips, my right lower eyelid, and under my left ankle. I knew exactly the wish he was talking about.

Déjà vu.

I time traveled back to the balloon launch.

What did you wish for?

I wish for an adventure so big that I get to feel things I've never felt before, bigger things, more grown up things.

I sighed, turning to look directly at Grief for the first time. I was partly surprised he didn't disappear. Underneath his hood, the Shadow's face morphed into Teddy's.

Be careful what you wish for.

"I guess I got my wish. Now I wish I could take it back."

You can't take it back now. So tell me now, if that balloon up there has more wish left in it, what do you REALLY want? Teddy's mouth formed Grief's words, in Teddy's voice.

"I wish to know the WHOLE of being human," I said out loud. This time I knew my voice and mouth formed the words into real sound. "All of it, even the ugly parts," I said, looking Teddy/Grief right in the eyes.

As you wish, Teddy/Grief said in his own voice, but with Teddy's twinkle in his eye.

And then the twinkle turned to fog, and Teddy's face returned to Grief's darkness.

There is some ugliness in this world that no one should ever have to witness, Grief/Teddy said with a heavy shadow in his voice.

"I know that now."

I wish for you, Alex, that you may always find the beautiful inside the ugly.

I turned my gaze back to the majestic tree.

There is always ALWAYS more than what you see with your eyes or hear with your ears. His voice sounded like Mr. Weismann now.

When you open your senses, dear Alex, and expose the rawness of your being, like you are doing now, you see the Whole.

A cold hand on my back pushed me closer to the tree. I felt her warmth pull me into her embrace. I wrapped my arms around her trunk, my chest and belly pressed right up to her, my left cheek resting on her knotted bosom.

And I sobbed.

My unzipping opened, but this time it wasn't down my back. It started at the tender divot space behind my left earlobe, and twisted down the side of my neck to the very similar divot space at the bottom of my throat. It felt like an unraveling rope, but it changed

171

at the notch at the bottom of my throat. The giant knot that was there didn't just untie, it exploded like a bursting water balloon.

Did I just spill sounds out of my throat all over the tree?

Was it all the tears I hadn't yet cried?

Were they held there in that knot just waiting for a way out?

When the last bit of juice emptied out, my throat felt raw, exposed, like it had been subjected to a cheese grater. Then Grief pushed me a little closer toward the tree, or maybe the tree pulled me in tighter. A piece of bark pierced the notch at the bottom of my throat, and I felt sliced open all the way down to the bottom of my sternum. Only this time, instead of my insides spilling out, I felt more like thin layers peeled open. Thousands of petal-soft, paper-thin layers of tissue blossomed open like a flower begging for sunlight.

But the sunlight was the tree's life force.

And she poured into me.

It was brighter than sunlight.

It was glittery, and shimmery, and sparkly, and warm, and sticky, and smooth, and vibrant. Electrically vibrant.

I felt as though I had plugged my heart into the source-socket of vitality, and this ancient tree-being rapidly replaced all the blood in my heart with her tree-light effervescent life force. I don't know how long I stayed there, enmeshed with the tree, floating in the boundary-less dream state.

CHAPTER TWENTY-THREE

Side B - The Sun

When I finally opened my eyes, my arms still wrapped around the trunk of the tree, I tilted my chin up toward the sky. A single ray of sunlight pierced through a cloud, made its way through the leaves and landed right on my face.

It was time.

I had to go up.

The tree seemed to push me away from her, and as I stepped away, the peeled layers sealed themselves right back up, seamlessly. I felt full, whole, contained . . . and safe. I strapped my backpack over my shoulders and backed away far enough that I could see the whole tree fort. It wasn't just a fort anymore. It was a full treehouse. She held it, perfectly framed by her uplifted branches, nestled into the center of her bosom.

The tree fort itself was beautiful in its own way. While I knew that in the few days since Teddy's death my brothers had spent countless hours working on it, I had no idea the magic they had constructed with their craftsmanship.

I remembered the real ladder leading to the front porch, and the rope ladder leading to the trap door. But so much more had changed since that night of Teddy's kiss. The railing on the porch now had perfectly spaced spokes with cargo-net ropes swizzled between them. No one could fall from this treehouse, ever again. Dangling from the roof, next to the wind chimes, hung a pot of purple and white petunias. One of Mr. Weismann's gnomes guarded the front door with a sheepish little grin peeking between his grey mustache and beard. The best part was the wood-burned lettering in the center rung of the ladder, just above my eye level.

Persephone
Est. 1985

As a toddler, my favorite bedtime story had been Shel Silverstein's *The Giving Tree*. The first time my mom read the book to me, I asked her why the tree in the story didn't have a name. It didn't seem to bother me that the boy didn't have a name, but I was really concerned that the tree should have a name. I was obsessed with finding the perfect name for the tree. For years, Mom and I tried on different names. April. Susannah. Trinity. Judith. Amber. But none of them stuck. Then one day, in fourth grade, while studying Greek mythology in school, I found it. Persephone. The goddess of spring and nature, and the underworld. I used a purple marker to change her name on every page of my copy of *The Giving Tree*. The name Persephone was perfect because she gave everything of herself, even giving herself to death, for the boy.

I traced my fingers through the carved, black lettering before gripping the whole ladder rung in my hand. My fingers fell onto more lettering on the top edge. I had to step up onto the first rung to read what it said.

In loving memory of Teddy James ~ 1973-1985

I gulped and stepped back down. In a flash, I was five years old, standing at the bottom of the high dive ladder at the community swimming pool. I knew I wanted to go up. I knew I *needed* to go up. Like the high dive, I knew it was perfectly safe . . . now. And that there was really no way I could fall like Teddy did. I knew that if I didn't go up, I would regret it.

Fear paralyzed me.

Deep breath.

Curling my barefoot toes around the lip of the bottom rung with the weight of my backpack anchoring me, I gripped the wood-burned rung in both hands, and shifted my weight to pull my foot from the ground to the second rung.

Another deep breath.

Anxiety bubbled up from my belly to my chest.

I shifted my weight again, and lifted my foot to the third rung.

Deep breath.

And so I climbed.

A deep breath with every step.

I felt as though I was growing up with each step. From the five-year-old at the bottom of the diving board, to an eight-year-old riding the big kids' roller coaster at Valley Fair, to a 10-year-old writing in purple marker. By the time both my feet were on top of

Persephone's name plate and my hands held the railing of the porch, the feelings inside me shifted.

I wasn't anxious, or nervous, or scared anymore.

I was excited.

When I got to the top, I found the spot on the porch where Teddy and I dangled our legs over Excalibur. I sat down cross-legged with my backpack in my lap and looked through the rope railing down at the shrine I had made for Teddy, his pictures framing his name.

I heard him laughing.

My friendly ghost.

What's so funny, Teddy?

EVERYTHING!

I pulled the Walkman out of my backpack, put on the headphones, and flipped the tape to side B, pressing play. The tape started, but the music took a moment to click on.

Let's Go Crazy - Prince
Always stay happy, Alex. No matter what, you can always, always find a reason to be happy.

When Prince's voice crooned over organ tones, a big, familiar lump pushed up to the top of my throat and got stuck at the back of my tongue. It almost closed up my whole throat. A deep grumbling pressed against the bottom of the lump. About halfway through the song, as if on cue with the music, the lump just sort of fell out of my mouth.

Not a sob.

More of a croak, like a giant frog. A sound that had never come out of me before, ever. I half expected to see an actual frog land on my lap and hop away. With the lump gone, my throat wide open, I erupted in laughter.

Cry-laughing.

At first, it was fits and starts of awkward giggles. They weren't consistent, just sort of randomly popping and erupting. It felt like effervescent bubbles popping behind my trachea, but they got bigger, and eventually felt like mini-balloons popping inside my lungs. Then they turned into what felt like bubble gum pops blowing off my lips. And before I realized it, full-on belly laughter tumbled out of me.

I got up off the floor and danced to the beat of Prince singing about life, and death, and living. And I laughed, at the top of my lungs and the bottom of my belly.

I laughed.

Until I wasn't laughing anymore.

At the end of the song, my laughter became sobs once again. I collapsed to the floor and banged my fists on the floor like a toddler in a temper tantrum, while Prince's guitar solo wailed with me.

Laugh-crying.

But Teddy wouldn't let me wallow for long.

Girls Just Wanna Have Fun - Cyndi Lauper
Alex, you should ALWAYS walk in the sun!

Cyndi Lauper's squeaky voice and the bubble-popping sounds in the soundtrack forced what few lumps were left in my chest to explode into a ricochet of laughs. The music pulled me up off the floor and spun me around, laugh-singing, twirl-spinning, hiccup-giggling all at the same time.

Life is too short, Alex. You gotta have FUN!

When the song ended, I pushed stop on the Walkman and sat cross-legged again on the floor of the treehouse porch, mainly to catch my breath.

Lucky Star - Madonna

Because at night, the stars are bright, and stars are just far away suns. Plus, I had to include this 'cuz it's your favorite.

I dug the binoculars out of my backpack and sunk onto my back in the center of the tree fort floor. As I listened to my favorite Madonna song, I focused the binoculars through the one skylight of the tree fort to look up through the leaves, pretending the purple balloon caught in the high up branches was a lucky star.

By the time I had caught my breath, the next song came on.

I Wanna Know What Love Is - Foreigner

Alex, remember this, the best storylines are ALWAYS about love. Isn't this what life is all about, really knowing what love is?

I let the binoculars drop to the floor as I laid flat, staring up at nothing in particular.

Was this Teddy's way of saying he loved me?

While my vision remained unfocused on the leaves and sunlight, my mind focused in on the memory of Teddy's kiss. I wanted to relive every moment of that kiss while listening to this song. The heavy lump lodged itself back in my throat and brought with it more bullfrog croaks. Only this time they weren't foreign, and certainly not the least bit funny anymore. Rather, they were groans; forceful, heavy, guttural groans.

I love him too.

Sunglasses at Night - Corey Hart
I think wearing your sunglasses at night is about making your own sun. Keep writing your storylines, Alex, they are your own sun.

Teddy had a way of finding alternate meanings in things that no one else saw. I always thought this song was about a man being cheated on by a woman, but he argued with me that the guy used the sunglasses to see things better, brighter.

Then, without thinking about it, I strapped the binoculars around my neck and went back out to the treehouse porch. Leaning on the railing, I looked through the binoculars towards to the street.

And then I saw it.

Magnified by both my tears and the binoculars.

The Stink House.

FLASH.

I needed sunglasses.

Rewind.

Tommy pulling the wisp of hair out of my face.

A knot in my stomach.

Did I cheat on Teddy without even knowing it?

Play.

Tommy's lips on mine.

The stiff awkwardness.

I dropped the binoculars onto my chest.

Stop.

A clear line of vision, from the tree fort to the Stink House.

Teddy had binoculars with him that day.

Did Teddy see me with Tommy on the stink house roof?

Rewind.

Did Teddy see Tommy kiss me?

Holy shit.

HOLY SHIT!!!!

Stop.

TEDDY SAW TOMMY KISS ME!

Is that why he fell?

Did Teddy think I liked Tommy and not him?

Did Teddy die because of me?

My throat hurt.

I didn't want to cry anymore.

And if I was completely honest with myself . . .

I didn't want to laugh anymore either.

I wanted to be done.

But I couldn't be done.

Not until the tape was done.

The Shadow pushed my finger back to the play button.

I couldn't be done.

Not until the tape was done.

Play.

Jump - Van Halen

Remember the first time we heard this song and we jumped, trying to hold onto that weightless feeling at the top of the jump? That weightless feeling, that's where the sun meets the happy. Don't ever forget that. Whenever you need a little happy, just jump.

As much as I didn't feel like I wanted to, I got up and jumped. I jumped with both feet all over the porch of the tree fort. Persephone danced with me, letting her branches and limbs quiver and give with each jump.

I lost control.

Exhilaration.

Euphoria.

I spun.

I jumped.

I head-banged and flipped my hair in a way that I knew would make Teddy proud.

And I bounced—

—right into the railing.

But Teddy didn't have a railing.

Gulp.

I leaned over the railing, looking down at the shrine I had made for Teddy on Excalibur's stump. I felt my heart beat louder and stronger and more alive than I had ever felt before.

Teddy was jumping when he died.

Teddy was ALIVE when he died.

And that was all I needed to know.

Acknowledgements

Writing is a deep exercise in solitude, and wouldn't be possible without my own host of angels, tizzy of faeries, and pleasure of pixies who support me from behind the scenes. To the high school students in my 2005 Creative Writing who listened to the early drafts of this book every day, thank you for paying attention and being interested even though we all knew you took the class as an easy elective. I hope you grew up to appreciate quality writing and a good story and all it has to teach. To my writing group, thank you for meeting me at coffee shops all across the Twin Cities and writing next to me without ever expecting to workshop my stuff. I wish for you all to find the joys of writing as I have. To my best friend and writing mentor, Megan, thank you for showing up for me time and again and walking next to me on this gnarly journey. To my editors, Laura and Sonnet, thank you for being the nit-picky detail-oriented mechanics police who polished this piece to a beautiful sheen. And lastly, thank you to my Hobbit, my husband, the love of my life, for gently pushing me to listen to the alter ego voices of my characters and pulling a depth out of the story that I wouldn't have otherwise found.

About the Author

In addition to publishing several books, TeriLeigh has been a high school teacher for at-risk youth, a yoga instructor, a Reiki Master, a chakra and aura reader, a life coach, and a shaman practitioner. For over a decade, she traveled across America guest presenting in yoga studios, corporate offices, schools, small businesses, and wellness venues. She has taught over 200,000 students, worked one-on-one with over 2000 clients, and presented in venues more than 20 states. Splitting her time between St. Paul Minnesota and the mountains of western Virginia, TeriLeigh founded and manages the Mindfulness Online Academy. She shares her life and passions with her husband, Neil, and two dogs, she calls her familiars.

Books by Teri Leigh

Mindfulness Online Academy Programs by TeriLeigh

Body Wisdom: Mindfulness in Healthy Posture & Mechanics

The Goldilocks Principle: A Practical Guide to the Chakras

The MOZI Method for Mindfulness

Yoga Wonderland: Adventures in Home Practice

Coaching with TeriLeigh

Body Wisdom: Mindfulness in Healthy Posture & Mechanics

The Goldilocks Principle: A Practical Guide to the Chakras

The Gift Inside the Wound: Mindfulness Through Trauma & Tragedy

The Hobbit and the Owl: MIndfulness of Couples

The MOZI Method for Mindfulness

Sukha's Way: A Mindful & Healthy Relationship with Food

Yoga Wonderland: Adventures in Home Practice